BEATITALES

80 FABLES ABOUT THE BEATITUDES FOR CHILDREN

JARED DEES

FORMATIVE FICTION

For more information visit jareddees.com.

Paperback: ISBN 978-1-7332048-0-4
eBook: ISBN 978-1-7332048-1-1

First Edition

For my girls.
I am very blessed.

CONTENTS

BLESSED ARE THOSE WHO HUNGER AND
THIRST FOR RIGHTEOUSNESS, FOR THEY WILL
BE FILLED

BLESSED ARE THE MERCIFUL, FOR THEY WILL
RECEIVE MERCY

INTRODUCTION

This morning, my daughter ate breakfast with her fingers in her ears. Yes, this makes it very difficult to eat toast. But she couldn't stand it any longer. Her older sister was lecturing her about compassion. My oldest daughter was trying her best to explain why her younger sister needed to be more compassionate.

To make matters worse, I interjected and tried to lecture her about lecturing her sister. There were a lot of lectures going on at breakfast this morning, and none of them seemed to be making an impact.

I realized that this moment was the perfect example of why stories teach us much better than what we traditionally think of as "teaching." A lecture is not the best way to teach. A lecture is not the best way to get through to someone. People don't like to be told what to do. Most of the time, we like discovering things on our own because we love our freedom to choose.

While receiving a lecture might feel like someone is trying to take away our freedom to choose, a story is welcomed as an opportunity to free us. Stories show us that we are not alone. Stories redefine the possible and the impossible. They help us see how others live in the world, which helps us realize how we can live, too.

When Jesus shared the Beatitudes with his disciples, he was not lecturing them. The Beatitudes were an invitation to his disciples to become a new kind of people. He was inviting them to understand what people are like in the Kingdom of God. These Beatitudes are not laws to follow but invitations to live differently or, in some cases, to embrace and accept the hidden benefits of a life that may otherwise be hard to enjoy.

Imagine if Jesus phrased the Beatitudes like this instead:

You're not poor enough. You're not sad enough. You're not meek enough. You're not hungry and thirsty enough. You're not merciful enough. You're not pure enough. You're fighting too much. You deserve to be persecuted.

He made factual statements rather than giving directives. He reassured his disciples that these seemingly unfortunate situations of life could actually be blessings. He told them that these situations could be a path toward happiness.

The problem is that most people in this world believe that the opposite is true. People avoid these states of life. No one wants to be poor. It hurts to mourn the loss of someone or something. We're told to speak up and be strong, not meek. There are so many restaurants and grocery stores around us that we never have a lack of food. The stories in the news speak of justice, not mercy. Purity is thought to be impossible. Persecution is avoided for the sake of being politically correct and inoffensive, and thus no one expresses what he or she truly believes.

The people of this world plug their ears to block out anyone who would make such absurd claims about striving to be poor, mournful, hungry, thirsty, merciful, pure, a peacemaker, or persecuted. And yet this is exactly what Jesus tells us to be. These Beatitudes are great mysteries, and meditating on their truths is time well spent.

It is one thing to know the meaning of each of the words in the Beatitudes, but it is another thing entirely to be able to understand how we can personally live them, too. A story helps us relate to someone who is living out these teachings. It helps us to apply these ways of living to our own lives, too. The stories in this book offer invitations, not directives, to a different way of life.

The stories are written in the form of fables and parables—genres meant to teach specific moral lessons. When we put ourselves in the shoes of the characters in a fable or parable, we come to understand more deeply how they learned (or failed to learn) a very important life lesson. Some of the people, animals, and objects in these stories are blessed. They are happy despite the conflicts and challenges they experience in the name of the truths that they embrace. Other characters you will encounter struggled because they did not learn to live these Beatitudes. By imagining what it would be like to be each one of these characters, we can make connections to our own lives and the way we seek happiness.

While you won't find Jesus' name in most of the stories, it is his life that provides the model by which any one of these characters would find comfort. He was poor. He mourned. He was meek and hungry and merciful and pure even under the most awful persecution leading up to his death. It is through him that we are blessed. It is my hope that through these stories, you will find his blessing, too.

I invite you to read and reflect on the stories in this book. I hope they challenge you to think about the way you are living your life today. They certainly challenge me to think deeply about the way I am living as a disciple in the world. They challenge me to seek God and his kingdom rather than the false promises of happiness that this world has to offer.

May God bless us in ways we may not even fully understand!

BLESSED ARE THE POOR IN
SPIRIT, FOR THEIRS IS THE
KINGDOM OF HEAVEN

THE WEALTHY LANDOWNER AND
THE HAPPY SERVANT

A wealthy landowner spent most of his days worrying about losing his great fortune.

He worried about the weather and about potential storms that could ruin his farm. He worried about other landowners, whose crops might be sold to his buyers instead of his own. He worried about his home and the many things that needed to be repaired. He also worried about his servants, in fear that they might run off and leave him with no one to help during the harvest.

As he pondered these thoughts, the landowner looked out the window of his large home and saw one of his servants. To his surprise, the man was smiling. He was so poor, yet so happy.

"How could this be?" the landowner said to himself.

He decided to confront the servant, asking him how he could be so happy when he had so little.

"Good sir, I have all that I need," the man replied.

"But can't you see this large house where I stay? Isn't this something you wish to have?" asked the landowner.

"You have given me a shelter with a roof to keep me

from the cold. What else should I want?" the servant said in reply.

"But I can serve great meals and share them with very important people. Do you not wish to have that as well?" asked the landowner.

"You have given me food each day for myself and for my family. None of us go hungry," said the servant.

"But look at all the amazing things I have bought with my money. Do you not wish to own such things as these?" asked the landowner.

"You have given me wages to buy the things we need to live a happy life," replied the servant.

At this last reply, the landowner suddenly realized the most valuable part of his wealth. It was not his house or the extravagant foods at his table. It was not the many things he could buy. It was in his ability to provide for others that his wealth had real value.

From that day forward, the landowner lived a much happier life. He did not worry about keeping his wealth safe. Instead, he spent his days buying only what he needed and giving the rest of his wealth to help others.

Blessed are the poor in spirit, for theirs is the kingdom of heaven.

THE HAPPY WORM

There was a small worm that went in search of a comfort-able home with good food to eat. After much traveling through the rocky ground (which was not good soil for a worm to live in), he saw a tree. The worm could see many luscious fruits hanging from the branches of the tree. He was very excited. He had found a home fitting for him to live in.

As he got closer, however, he started to run into other worms moving in the direction of the tree. There were hundreds of worms, and other bugs too, on their way to take up residence there.

Once he arrived, the fruit was already almost gone. The worm ate his fill, but before long the tree was mostly barren. It was still enough for him, though. He had wandered on a long and hard journey, and he wished to make this his home. A few leaves and a fruit now and then would be enough.

The other worms and bugs didn't feel this way. They got impatient and hungry. They decided they would move on in search of a better, more bountiful tree. They tried to convince the worm to join them. They described what it would be like to find another tree as full of fruit as this one had been.

But they could not convince him to go. As the others left, the worm looked around. He was almost entirely alone. There was more than enough room in the tree now for him and a few others and more than enough food to eat. He was quite content and glad he didn't let a desire for more get the best of him.

As for the other bugs, they continued to move from tree to tree, always searching for a better, more bountiful tree. The worm lived in the tree for the rest of his life, and he was very happy.

Blessed are the poor in spirit, for theirs is the kingdom of heaven.

THE TWO TRAVELERS

Two travelers each prepared for a pilgrimage to a holy festival. One traveler prepared day and night in the weeks leading up to the trip, collecting every tool or item he thought he would need to arrive safely at the destination. The other traveler packed lightly and took with him only what was necessary.

Each traveler set out on the same day and at the same time. It was a long journey. They met along the road and traveled together on the way. The first traveler wondered how his companion possibly expected to arrive without all the tools and supplies he himself had packed.

Then they realized they were lost.

The first traveler stopped to look through his many tools to help him find the way. It took a very long time to sort through his possessions to find the ones he needed.

The other traveler simply said a prayer and continued on the journey, trusting that God would help him find his way. He moved quickly, and before long he found the right path again. The first traveler eventually found his way, too, but he had to go backward and pick another road to get there.

Although the two travelers were now far apart, they both felt the extreme heat of the next day. It was exhausting and slowed them down. The traveler with few possessions was slowed only a little and was able to arrive at the festival. The first traveler, however, was overcome by heat and exhaustion from carrying so many things. He had to take many breaks along the way.

By the time the first traveler arrived, with his many possessions still intact, the festival was over. People were leaving. He saw his former companion leaving, too, and realized what he had done. He had placed his trust in his supplies rather than God.

Blessed are the poor in spirit, for theirs is the kingdom of heaven.

THE PRIDEFUL EXPLORER

A young man wanted to sail around the world. He was an explorer but also an inventor. He had created many tools to help him on his quest. He told people he wanted to be known as the greatest explorer and the greatest inventor of all time.

It took many years and many conversations, but he finally convinced the king to fund his journey and lend him a ship to sail on his adventure. The king wanted him to take with him an experienced captain who was well versed in the old ways of navigating the water. The king did not trust the young man's new inventions.

The young man scoffed at the idea. "Who needs experience when you have tools such as these?"

The young man did not follow the king's advice. He hired his own crew and began the journey, trusting in his own tools. For a little while, things went well. The inventions worked perfectly. They were well on their way around the world.

Then a terrible storm hit and the young explorer's tools malfunctioned. He and his crew survived the storm, but they were lost at sea. Without the tools and without an experienced captain to help them, they were doomed.

They continued to sail, though they did not know where they were until they saw a port in the distance. When they arrived at the port, they realized that they had not traveled very far at all. They were still in the kingdom from which they had come.

The king found out about their return and was angry. He took back his ship and banished the young man from the kingdom. The king gave his ship to another sailor who was willing to follow his advice. The young man was disgraced, never to explore again.

Blessed are the poor in spirit, for theirs is the kingdom of heaven.

THE SICK SON

There was a very sick boy who spent months in the hospital. His doctors tried using many medicines to heal him, but his health was only getting worse. He talked about heaven all the time, and this often made his parents cry.

His parents decided they wanted to give him the best day of his life. They wrote letters and sent messages to the young boy's favorite baseball player. They reached out repeatedly, trying to get him to visit the boy in the hospital.

The boy became sicker by the day, and the parents knew there wasn't a lot of time left. Finally, the baseball player agreed to meet with the boy.

The big day came, and the parents were so excited. They told their son they had a special surprise for him. Thinking about how much he would love the surprise made them very happy.

But something came up in the famous player's schedule, and he couldn't join them. He had to reschedule for the following week, but the parents knew there wouldn't be enough time.

They came to tell their son about what had happened. They thought he would be devastated.

He wasn't. He said to them, "Seeing the excitement on your faces made my day. It was the first time I've seen you smile in a very long time. That is what I needed the most."

The parents realized they had been trying to create a rich experience for the young boy, when all he really needed was the simple joy of seeing them smile.

They spent the next few days with their son, focusing on the little joys of each day. They smiled a lot, and the boy smiled too, right up to the day in which he was taken up to heaven.

Blessed are the poor in spirit, for theirs is the kingdom of heaven.

THE DAINTY DOG

There was a dainty dog that loved her new dog collar. The collar was lined with jewels and had a gold tag. When her owner took her for a walk, she held her head just a little higher so the other dogs could see the collar.

Not long after getting her this fancy collar, the dog's owner went away for the day. A neighbor came to let the dog out but forgot to lock the gate. The dog decided to take the opportunity to show off her new collar to the other dogs at the dog park.

She pushed open the gate and strutted down the road by herself, all the way to the dog park.

The gate to the dog park was shut. She waited for another dog and its owner to walk through the gate and then lunged toward the opening to sneak in behind them. Her collar got caught on the hinge, though, and she had to pull her head out to get into the park. When she got her head out, the gate went slamming shut, and the collar went flying through the air into some bushes.

It wasn't long before another owner came over to find her without a collar. "Is this anyone's dog?" yelled the owner, but there was no answer.

With no one there to claim her and no collar to show whose dog she was, the other owners were forced to call the dog pound. The pound soon picked her up from the park and put her in a cage.

The dog didn't like the pound or the cage. She thought that if she hadn't tried to show off her fancy collar, it wouldn't have gotten stuck in the bushes and she would have stayed home safe and sound. When her owner finally came to claim her, she vowed never to show off a collar or anything fancy about herself ever again.

Blessed are the poor in spirit, for theirs is the kingdom of heaven.

THE OLD CUP

A man had an old cup, which he loved to use and drink out of every day. It was a plain, simple cup without any fancy decorations. The color had faded over the years, and the writing on it could barely be seen. The old cup felt honored to be so loved by the man.

Eventually, the man's wife gave him a new cup to use and drink out of. At first, he didn't like the new cup and missed his old cup. But the new cup was much nicer and easier to hold, and the old cup had a few cracks and chips that embarrassed his wife. So the man placed the old cup in the back of the cupboard. He loved it too much to get rid of it.

The other cups in the cupboard thought that the old cup would be hurt. They knew they would be angry if they had been the man's favorite cup and were now left in the back of the cupboard.

But the old cup wasn't angry at all. In fact, it was very happy for the new cup. The old cup had spent so many years serving the man that it was quite content. It had many stories to share about the drinks it had held. This cheered up the other cups and helped them dream of being used by the man and his wife or one of the many guests they had over to the house. They all loved the old cup and liked to listen to its stories.

Blessed are the poor in spirit, for theirs is the kingdom of heaven.

THE NEW KID IN SCHOOL

A new boy arrived at school one day. He walked into class a little bit late. He had a smile on his face and was excited for the new day.

He wore a faded and frayed t-shirt. The boy was tall but skinny, and the shirt was quite baggy and hung slightly off his shoulder. Some of his new classmates began to whisper to each other about the boy and his shirt as he took his seat in the front of the room.

"Is there something you would like to share with the rest of the class?" the teacher said to the whispering children.

"No, ma'am," they replied.

At recess, the whispering continued. The kids looked with pity on the boy, but no one came to talk to him. In fact, the other kids avoided him as much as they could.

At the end of the day, the teacher called the boy over to her desk. "How was your first day? Did you make any new friends?"

"It was fine," said the boy. "I met a couple of new people."

"I noticed there was a lot of whispering and you didn't

play much at recess. Is there anything that anyone said to you that was hurtful? It's fine if you don't want to talk about it," said the teacher.

"No, not to my face, but I know they were talking about my shirt," he said, smiling.

The teacher frowned. "I wondered about that. Is there anything your family needs? There are organizations connected to the school that could help if your family is having financial trouble."

"Oh, we have plenty of money," said the boy. "I mean, we're not rich, but we do just fine."

The teacher looked down at the shabby t-shirt with a confused expression.

"This is my dad's lucky t-shirt," the boy said with a smile. "He's in the army. We moved here to be closer to family while he's deployed overseas. I miss him, but wearing this shirt today made me so happy. I really felt like he was with me."

"Why didn't you say anything to the other kids?" asked the teacher.

"We've moved around a lot. I'll make some friends and forget about the rest. It always takes time, no matter what. Can I go now?"

"Yes, go ahead," said the teacher.

The boy headed toward the door, where another student from the class was there waiting for him. One of them had a soccer ball in her hands. "You ready to go play with us?"

"C'mon, let's go!" said the boy.

Blessed are the poor in spirit, for theirs is the kingdom of heaven.

THE HIGH SCORE

A young teenage boy, who loved to play video games, had been playing a new online game called *Conquer the Kingdom*. He played it often and so well that his name was rising on the leaderboard as one of the best players in the game.

One afternoon, his mom had to go to an appointment and asked him to watch his little sister while he was gone. He often watched her at night when their parents went out on dates or in the afternoons when they had errands to run.

His homework was finished and he had nothing else to do. He decided to play his video game while his little sister played with dolls in her room.

It was by far his best performance in the game yet. He was on his way to breaking a new record in points. This would surely set him at the top of the leaderboard.

The game was intense. He had his headphones on and he was in the zone.

Then he had a sudden thought. What if something happened to his sister? How could he be sure she was okay when he was so focused on playing this game? He started to worry about her. He loved the little girl very much.

Even though he was just about to break the record for most points scored, he took off his headset and set the game aside. He knew his sister was more important than a high score. He walked upstairs to his sister's room to make sure she was okay.

She was fine. She was playing with her dolls very quietly. "Do you want to play with me?" she asked.

The boy smiled. "Sure," he said.

"But don't you want to finish your game?" she asked him.

"Nah," said the boy. "I can always play it another time. Let's play your game instead."

Blessed are the poor in spirit, for theirs is the kingdom of heaven.

THE NO. 2 PENCILS

A large box of standard No. 2 pencils sat patiently in a classroom closet, waiting for the students to arrive. Each of these pencils dreamed of the many great creations they would make with the kids once school began.

The first day of school finally came, and the kids poured into the classroom. School had started, but the pencils remained in the box. The kids were all using decorative pencils with flowers, superheroes, cartoons, and colorful designs instead. These pencils had big, fancy erasers, too.

The No. 2 pencils wondered if the students would ever use them. How could plain pencils ever be chosen over the beautiful and decorative pencils that the students liked to use? Still, the pencils knew their purpose. They were just as useful as any pretty pencil, and they waited patiently.

One day, there came a new student in school, who arrived without any pencils or paper or any supplies. She seemed sad that she had nothing to use in class.

So the teacher went back to the closet and picked up the box of No. 2 pencils. She gave it to the new student to use in class.

She was so grateful to have her very own set of pencils. She made many great creations and finished many difficult assignments with the help of these pencils. She was so grateful to have them that she didn't mind the plain brown color on the sides. She was just happy to have her own set of pencils. The pencils were happy to help her, too.

Blessed are the poor in spirit, for theirs is the kingdom of heaven.

BLESSED ARE THOSE WHO
MOURN, FOR THEY WILL BE
COMFORTED

THE LOST BIRD

There was a great storm blowing through the forest.

In that forest was a tree with a nest, a mother bird, and her baby bird. The baby bird did not yet know how to fly.

The storm blew very hard until it carried the baby bird out of its nest and far away from its mother. When the storm ended, the baby bird found itself somewhere it had never been before. It thought it would never see home and its mother again.

The bird cried and cried until a deer heard the bird and came to see what was the matter.

The bird explained what happened, and the deer felt sorry for it. "Baby bird, climb on my back and we will find your home." The deer knelt down so that the bird could climb on top of its back, and the baby bird held on tight with its talons.

The deer bolted around the forest, looking for the bird's mother. The baby bird chirped as loud as it could, calling for her.

They searched for days without finding the little bird's home. The bird was ready to give up. "I've lost her forever," it said, and began to cry once more.

The deer comforted the bird, telling it that they would stay together no matter what. The deer would be the bird's new family.

The bird's tears became a mix of joy and sadness. It cried for the loss of its mother and also cried out of joy for finding a new friend.

Then the bird heard something. It was its mother. She heard the crying and came to find her baby from a long distance away.

The baby bird was very happy. They had found its mother, and the baby bird had also found a friend.

Blessed are those who mourn, for they will be comforted.

THE LAMP AND THE LIGHT BULB

A family brought home a new lamp for their living room. The lamp was excited to be in a new home.

The mother found a great place for the lamp to sit, and the father found a nice light bulb to place within it.

Together, the lamp and the light bulb filled the room with light and witnessed many great moments with the family. They lit the room for family parties. They lit the room for the baby's first steps. They lit the room for quiet reading time for the adults.

Just when the lamp thought it couldn't be happier, the light bulb burned out. The lamp was devastated. It could no longer light the room without the help of this special light bulb.

The light bulb lost its light but not its love for the lamp. It comforted the lamp, saying, "Do not weep. We have shared and served in so many great memories. It has been a good life, and in my place you will find another. This is just the way of things. Thank you, lamp, for all that we have shared together."

Though the lamp was sad, it knew the light bulb was

right. It took comfort in the many great memories. It was very hard to say good-bye.

When the new light bulb was installed, the lamp was still sad, but it welcomed the new bulb, greeting it with affection and anticipation for the many new memories they would now make together.

Blessed are those who mourn, for they will be comforted.

THE LONE TURTLEDOVE

A princess locked herself in a steep tower in the castle. She wished to speak to no one, not even the king. She was deeply pained by the loss of a prince who died in battle while they were betrothed.

The king and the servants tried to comfort her but could not get her to come out of her misery. Soon, the king became angry and upset with her. He didn't understand why she was still so sad. He pleaded with her to come out. He and his servants tried everything, but all their trying only made her feel worse.

She was alone, and that was the way she wanted it. Her only companion during this time was a bird. A turtledove would come visit her each morning, landing on the windowsill of the tower.

The bird would visit each day and sing a soft, cooing call. It was a sad sound. It reminded the princess of the sound of her own crying call for her lost husband.

"Are you mourning the loss of another bird, dear turtledove?" she asked. "You are alone, aren't you? I know your pain."

The turtledove returned to be with her each day. Its

mere presence warmed the heart of the princess. The princess would cry and the turtledove would coo. Sometimes the princess would feed the bird, but it rarely ate.

This went on for a long time until the bird arrived one day and started to eat the food that the princess gave to it. It ate more and more each day and soon was singing to the princess with a comforting song. It made the princess feel better to watch the turtledove improve.

Finally, one day the turtledove came and sang a beautiful melody that lifted up the heart of the princess. With one last long look at her, the bird flew away. The princess thought she could hear the voice of another bird singing in the distance, as well.

"Thank you," she said to the bird. Then, for the first time in a long time, she opened the door to her room and went to join the kingdom.

Blessed are those who mourn, for they will be comforted.

THE MOTHER AND HER PUPPIES

A mother dog gave birth to a litter of puppies. She loved and cared for these little dogs for weeks until strange new people came to visit them.

One of these visitors picked up one of the puppies and took it away to live with another family. Then another family came to take one of the puppies, then another and another until only one puppy remained.

The mother dog was sad to lose so many of her puppies, and she didn't want to lose this last one, either. Then a little girl came and picked up that little puppy. She hugged it so tightly and looked on it lovingly.

The little girl turned to the mother and said, "I am going to take such good care of him. He is going to be the happiest puppy on earth. You don't have to worry one bit about him, okay? Thank you for such a beautiful little puppy. He is just the most amazing gift ever in the world."

This pleased the mother dog. She was sad to lose her puppies but glad to know they would be in the loving hands of people who cared for them.

Blessed are those who mourn, for they will be comforted.

THE MOURNING MOON

The moon was in mourning. It was sad because it never got to see the sun. Whenever the moon came out, the sun fled. It never stayed for the moon to see it.

This made the moon so sad one night that it decided to stop shining.

The people on earth shouted to the moon, "Where has your light gone?"

The moon said back, "I can no longer light up the night. I want to see the sun, but it flees my presence again and again."

"But moon," they shouted back, "we will miss you without your light in the night. We love to look at your beauty. You help us dream of things beyond ourselves. The sun may give us the light of the day, but we cannot look at it as we look at you. Please give us your light and shine throughout the night!"

The moon thought for a moment and realized for the first time that it was important to the people. It realized how they relied on it to give light to the night. It realized that it inspired people who looked upon its light.

The moon was filled with joy once more and shed light during the night for all to see.

Blessed are those who mourn, for they will be comforted.

THE HONORABLE KNIGHT

There was once a knight who sought honor above all else. He was dedicated to developing his skill as a soldier and preparing for the greatest feats in battle. He wanted nothing more than to win great battles and earn the high esteem of the people of the kingdom.

One day, a battle was waged unlike any he had seen before. Thousands of men fought all across the fields on foot. The knight was then called upon to join the other knights on horseback in the fray.

He fought valiantly and accomplished a great many deeds to earn him the admiration of the knights around him. But the battle was not leaning in their favor. More and more men fled in retreat, but not this knight. He fought even more bravely to defend his honor and the honor of his kingdom. Many men fought by his side, inspired by his courage.

He fought and he fought, but it was to no avail. The knight fell in battle and was knocked unconscious.

Many hours later he awoke, and the battle was over. He stood up but was very dizzy from the blow to his head. He was disappointed because he thought it was his fate to die in battle and earn the honor he had sought for his whole life.

Then he caught sight of the battlefield. There lay many men wounded or dying. Tears filled his eyes, not because of his dishonorable loss in battle but for the sorrow and suffering he saw all around him. His heart ached for these men who had fought so bravely and sacrificed all for the sake of the kingdom.

From that day forward, he did not fight to be honored by others but to honor these men who had died for the kingdom. They remained with him always, and the pain he felt for them never left him.

Blessed are those who mourn, for they will be comforted.

THE COLORING BOOK

A family brought home a brand new coloring book from the store. This coloring book was so excited to share its many creative designs and for the children to color neatly within its lines.

On the very next day, the toddler of the family opened up the coloring book and scribbled on almost all of the pages.

The coloring book felt ruined! Who would color in it now?

Truly, the older kids did not want to color it anymore. They always chose another coloring book without scribbles to use instead. This made the coloring book feel very sad and worthless.

Days went by and then months and years, and this coloring book was never opened nor used by the children.

Then one day the family went on a road trip with a very long car ride. The mother of the family had packed up a collection of coloring books for the car ride. She must have made a mistake, because she grabbed a stack of used coloring books, including the scribbled-in one, instead of all the brand new, clean ones.

At first, the older kids discarded the books. In fact, they didn't want to color in them at all. This made that coloring book so very sad.

The youngest of the family, who was older than a toddler now, picked up the old coloring book. "What happened to this one?" she asked.

Her siblings told her that she had scribbled all over it when she was little.

"Oh," she said. "That's okay. I guess I will have to finish what I started."

The little girl spent the rest of the time in the car coloring either over or with her scribbles. Soon she made each one of those scribbled pages into beautifully colored designs that made the coloring book very proud to have been colored in by the youngest sibling.

Blessed are those who mourn, for they will be comforted.

THE DYING DOG

A boy had a dog that was getting pretty old. He and his dog used to run through the fields together behind their house, but now the dog was slow to follow and limped when he walked.

So the boy would play games with him that didn't require a lot of running and jumping. He loved that dog so much.

The boy's parents were very worried. They knew that the dog could die any day now. They were afraid that it would devastate the boy.

After dinner one day, they sat him down to tell him that the dog was close to death. They told him how very sad this made them and that it was okay for him to be sad, too.

The boy looked at them, confused. "I know that," he said. "Mom and Dad, it's okay for you to be sad. It makes me sad, too, but I'm going to make the most of this time with him while I can. We're having more fun now than we ever did when he was a young dog. Let's go and enjoy him, okay?"

This really comforted the parents. Their son was right.

They were so worried about their dog dying that they didn't enjoy the time they had with him while he was still living.

The dog lived for a few more weeks, and the whole family loved every minute of their time with him.

When he passed away, all of them were in tears, but they were comforted by the many great memories they had shared with him, right up to the last moment.

Blessed are those who mourn, for they will be comforted.

THE FRIEND IN NEED

There were two girls in school who were absolutely insepa-rable. They ate lunch together every day. They played together at recess and sat next to each other on the bus. They dressed alike. They talked alike. And they even looked alike, except one of the girls was tall and the other was short. They were best friends for life.

Until one morning, the taller girl stepped onto the bus to find her friend's backpack blocking the seat next to her.

"I want to sit alone today," said her friend. She stared out the window.

The taller girl could not get her to speak, but she didn't get angry and tried not to feel hurt. She knew something was wrong, and she wanted to help. She decided to wait until lunch.

At lunch, her friend continued to want to sit alone. She was silent and moved her lunch tray to another seat far away from her friend or anyone else.

The taller girl still didn't get upset or angry. She gave her friend some space, seeing that she needed it right now.

Finally, on the bus ride home, the shorter girl still blocked the seat next to her with her backpack. The taller girl turned to a boy sitting across the aisle. "Would you mind if I sat here today?"

The boy shrugged his shoulders and said, "Sure."

She sat down across the aisle from her friend.

"I'm going to sit over here. You don't have to talk, but I want you to know that I'm here for you. Whatever it is, I'm here when you need me, and I want you to know that."

Her friend turned and had a tear in her eye. She mouthed the words, "Thank you."

The bus drove on until finally the shorter girl did speak. She took a deep breath, turned to her friend, and said, "It's my mom. She's sick. I didn't want to talk about it. I just can't even think about it."

"I'm so sorry," said her friend. "I'm here for you whenever you are ready."

Blessed are those who mourn, for they will be comforted.

THE TREE SPROUT

A small sprout of a tree finally grew its first leaves. The tree was so proud of itself. It looked to all the other tall trees that had many leaves and dreamed of becoming like them some day. All through the summer, the tree sprout proudly displayed its beautiful green leaves. There weren't many, but the tree was happy to have them.

Then the days started to get colder and colder. The color of the leaves turned from a bright green to a beautiful red, then a bright yellow. This surprised the sprout, but it knew that the leaves were still beautiful.

Then the color of the leaves turned from yellow to brown, and the leaves started to wither away. The leaves crumbled and fell to the ground. The little tree sprout was devastated. How could it possibly grow into a great tree, now that its leaves were all gone?

The great trees around the sprout took notice. "Why do you mourn?" asked one of the trees nearby.

"Because the few leaves I have are gone. I am barren and awful to look at," said the sprout.

Another large tree spoke now to comfort the sprout.

"Little tree, yes, this is a sad day. The leaves are gone, and you are right to mourn their loss, for they were beautiful."

"What will I do now? I have nothing," said the sprout.

"Be patient," said the big tree. "In time, new leaves will sprout in the place of the old, and you will grow again, and more leaves will join what was lost. This is the necessary way of things. Be strong during the long winter months, and you will find new life afterward."

The sprout trusted the great trees. It had no other choice. So it mourned the loss of its leaves. Soon it noticed that the other trees lost their leaves, too. There were lost leaves everywhere, and it was good to know that the sprout wasn't alone.

The winter passed and then spring came again. The sprout no longer mourned in loss. Instead, new life began to make an appearance on its branches. New leaves arrived, and the sprout grew into a little tree with many more leaves on its small branches.

Year after year, the tree mourned the loss of its beautiful leaves, but it always looked ahead to the new life that would be born in place of what was lost.

Blessed are those who mourn, for they will be comforted.

BLESSED ARE THE MEEK,
FOR THEY WILL INHERIT
THE EARTH

THE THREE KINGDOMS

There was a land with three kingdoms. The first and greatest kingdom was full of strong warriors who won many heroic battles by might and sword.

The second kingdom was smaller than the first and valued intellect over strength. They were cunning and strong in intelligence.

The third and smallest kingdom was neither strong nor superior in intelligence. The people of this kingdom valued peace over war. They were satisfied with what they had and not eager to prove their superiority by might or mind.

One day, the king of the first kingdom said, "We will conquer the other kingdoms and rule the land!"

The king of the second kingdom heard of these intentions. It made him angry, and he and prepared for battle. He made an intelligent plan to defeat the strong warriors who would attack them.

The war between these two kingdoms lasted many years, with the first kingdom attacking with might and the second countering with the mind. Years passed, until there were very few people in either kingdom left to fight.

The kings said to themselves, "We have fought for

many long years, and now we are poor and hungry. We must go to the third kingdom for assistance against our enemy."

The kings arrived at the castle of the third kingdom at the same time, both with small armies who were weary with battle.

The third king saw the armies and called them all to a council of the three kingdoms. There the kings discussed the future.

"You will declare a truce," said the third king. "My kingdom, which is now plentiful in resources, will be able to provide assistance for you. You will each hand over control of your kingdoms to me as we rebuild for the both of you. We will ensure that peace remains for the many years to come."

Both kings thought of their many hungry and wounded subjects. They felt they had no other choice than to agree. Thus, the third king inherited all three kingdoms, ruling over all the land forever.

Blessed are the meek, for they will inherit the earth.

THE ANGRY CAPTAIN

A ship captain wanted everything on his ship to be perfect. When the men under his direction made mistakes, he became furious. Some of the time, he would be so angry with them that he would leave them at the next port and go on the voyage without them.

This happened again and again until the men of the ship hated the captain. Most of them gladly welcomed the chance to be left at the next port. Soon, the captain had a very bad reputation, and very few sailors wanted to work for him, no matter how much he paid them.

On one particular voyage, he sailed with only five ship-mates to serve him. The captain had to do much of the work himself.

It wasn't long before the captain made a mistake. He was dumbfounded. He had always done everything perfectly. He had never made a mistake before.

The crew, however, did not get angry with the captain. They fixed the mistake and never said a word of it. These particular men were so hardworking and focused that they did not hate the captain at all for his mistake and the many mistakes that he made throughout the voyage.

The captain saw how these men treated him with kind-ness, and something changed within him. He had much more patience with the men, and he and the crew worked together to reach their final destination, an island that very few people had visited.

It was here that they found a buried treasure, which the captain had searched for years to find.

Instead of giving the men a small part of the booty, he split it all evenly with them, making each one of them very, very rich.

Blessed are the meek, for they will inherit the earth.

THE SILENT DAUGHTER

Two parents were very worried about their young daughter. She wouldn't (or, they thought, maybe couldn't) speak. She was a happy child, and healthy, too, but she never spoke. She grew older but remained silent. Other kids her age started speaking words and then in full sentences. This little girl never said a thing.

She didn't talk, but she didn't cry, either. She never seemed to get upset. She rarely cried out or threw temper tantrums like other kids her age.

The parents took her to doctor after doctor, and none of them could get her to talk. They did brain scans but couldn't find anything out of the ordinary.

The parents were still worried, but they continued to love her like they would love any other child. They cared for her, and she made them happy.

The parents discovered over time that their little girl loved to be outdoors. She was always full of joy when she could behold the view of beautiful scenery. She seemed to see things that even her parents didn't notice.

The girl became a gifted artist. She never spoke, but she was able to communicate very well through her art.

Most of all, she could depict the beauty of the earth better than anyone her parents had ever seen. She always carried with her a calmness and attachment to the awesomeness of nature.

Blessed are the meek, for they will inherit the earth.

THE OLD DOG'S YARD

There was an old dog that loved to run through the yard of his home. He had the yard all to himself until one day his owner brought home a new dog. She was still just a puppy and she had lots of energy. She wanted to play in the yard too, but the old dog didn't like that at all. He growled at her and chased her down when she ran through the yard.

The old dog became so angry that he even tried to bite the puppy when she came too close. She didn't fight back at all. She let the old dog attack. The owner saw this and locked the old dog in a cage. He didn't want him to hurt their new puppy.

So the old dog was forced to watch the new dog run happily through his yard while he sat jealously looking on in a very cramped cage.

Blessed are the meek, for they will inherit the earth.

THE CALM COWS

There were two families that each owned cows. The cows roamed freely across the valley floor. They loved living there and got along very nicely with one another, even though they were owned by different families.

The families, however, were always fighting. They argued daily over the land of the valley. They tried to divide the land evenly, but no one ever seemed to be satisfied.

The sons of one of the families started to build a fence to mark off their plot of land and keep in only their cows. The cows were sad to be separated, but they listened to their owners.

The other family saw them constructing the fence, and the brothers came to confront them. The argument escalated and turned into a fight, and one of the brothers was mortally wounded. He died three days later.

The cows watched from a distance. They roamed away from the fighting and kept themselves safe.

The brother's death began a great war between the two families. They fought and killed each other over the land until each of them was either dead or too sad to stay there any longer. The families were both forced to move away.

All that remained after the feud was the cows. The families couldn't manage them any longer, so they were left to roam free. The cows continued to get along quite nicely in their wide-open valley.

Blessed are the meek, for they will inherit the earth.

THE REMODELED KITCHEN

The kitchen in a certain house had become old, sad, and rundown. The appliances were breaking, and the cupboards and countertops were falling apart.

So the owners of the house decided to remodel and improve the kitchen, making it beautiful once again. People came to visit and marveled at the new and improved kitchen.

At night, the kitchen started to boast to the other rooms in the house about how beautiful it had become.

The other rooms became jealous of the newly redesigned kitchen. They were starting to feel old and rundown, too.

One room, however, didn't feel this way. The bathroom had been remodeled multiple times. The bathroom stayed quiet for a long time as the kitchen boasted of its beauty.

Then the bathroom reminded the kitchen to be careful about boasting. "No matter how many times we are updated, dear kitchen, remember that a kitchen is still a kitchen and a bathroom is still a bathroom. You will grow old and worn down again, but old or new, your purpose will remain the same."

The people remodeled many of the other rooms in the house, but each room always remembered the bathroom's reminder to stay true to its own purpose no matter how new or old it had become.

Blessed are the meek, for they will inherit the earth.

THE LOUD WASHING MACHINE

A family had a new washing machine and a new dryer. The dryer was very calm and quiet. Indeed, the people had to turn the volume up on the signal so they knew when it was finished drying the clothes.

The washer was not so quiet. It wanted to aggressively clean all the clothes that the people entrusted to its care. The washer would shake almost the entire house so that everyone would know it was getting the clothes as clean as can be. It liked being heard for hard work.

The kids of the family played outside in the mud one day, and the parents put their dirty clothes in the washing machine. The washing machine knew it was up to the task and began a heavy wash cycle. It shook and it spun and it gave all its power to clean the clothes. It shook itself so much that it sprung a leak, and water went everywhere.

The family had to replace that washer. They loved the clean clothes, but they didn't love the noise or the shaking. They found instead a washing machine that was efficient but quiet, like the dryer.

Blessed are the meek, for they will inherit the earth.

THE THREE STEREO SPEAKERS

A store had a new line of stereo speakers that were ready for sale for people to buy and use to listen to music in their homes. The storeowner lined up all the speakers on the front table for shoppers to see.

There were three kinds of speakers. One was large and loud. Another was very fancy and beautiful to see. The third speaker system was plain and not quite as loud as the others.

Customers came in and tested the speakers out. Some turned up the volume as high as it could go for each one. These people loved the loud sounds. So they bought the loud speakers.

Other customers liked the look of the fancy speakers. They were more interested in how the speakers looked than how loud they could get. These people bought the fancy speakers.

Day after day, the little speakers sat unsold in the store. It was feared that they wouldn't sell at all.

Then things started to change. The people who bought the loud speakers came in to demand a refund. The speakers had burst and broke because the volume had been turned up too loud.

Then people brought in the fancy speakers, demanding their money back. The shiny gloss on the speakers wore off quickly from the vibrations of the sound, and the speakers now looked awful.

So it was that all those people purchased the little speakers instead. These speakers weren't too loud and they weren't too fancy, but they worked well and brought beautiful music into the lives of the people who listened with them.

Blessed are the meek, for they will inherit the earth.

THE MOUSE WARRIOR

There once was a mouse that served in the lion king's army. Everyone laughed at the mouse, for he was small and easily defeated in battle. Even so, the mouse worked hard and served loyally.

Every year, the kingdoms of the jungle each selected one animal to fight in a great tournament. The lion king selected this small mouse as his champion. "I trust in you, my young mouse. Do you trust in me?" said the king.

"But, sir, I am not strong in battle. I am not strong enough to fight on your behalf," replied the mouse.

"Trust in me," is all the response that the king gave him.

The mouse entered the tournament in humble service of the king. The king's confidence in him helped him overcome his fear. Others came to the tournament with pride and confidence in themselves, while the mouse came with confidence in his king.

The mouse won battle after battle by letting his opponents defeat themselves. The rhinoceros charged the mouse but missed. He ran his long horn into a tree and couldn't get it out. The elephant tried to stomp the mouse, but he missed, too, and broke his ankle when he stomped too hard. The monkey tried to swing his way up to chase after the mouse to the top of a tree, but he was too heavy for the branches and fell to the ground.

Finally, the mouse was in the last match, against the tiger.

"The rhinoceros, the elephant, and the monkey defeated themselves, but I will not be so foolish. Come and fight me, little mouse," the tiger said.

The mouse didn't know what to do. He could not face the tiger directly in combat; he would surely be eaten.

He remembered the confidence his king had given to him. Setting aside his fear once more, he ran toward the tiger, yelling, "For the king!"

The tiger was surprised but didn't stay still. He saw his chance and perched himself on his hind legs, ready to lunge at the mouse when it came near.

Then the mouse stopped. He was just a few feet away from the tiger, but the mouse was small and just out of reach. The mouse stood there, staring at the tiger in silence.

The tiger, confused at first, didn't waste much time. He jumped toward the mouse with his great mouth open wide and his many sharp teeth. The mouse stood patiently, then jumped back at the last moment.

There below his feet was a small, gray stone. The mouse was so quick that the tiger thought the stone was the mouse. He bit down as hard as he could. The stone became stuck in his mouth, and the tiger was defeated.

The mouse had won the tournament

He returned to the kingdom with great honor.

"Hooray for the mouse!" shouted the animals of the kingdom.

The king rewarded the mouse's trust in him with a high place in his court. The mouse helped the king rule over all the land for the many years that followed.

Blessed are the meek, for they will inherit the earth.

THE OLD COCKROACH

There was a great, old cockroach who was a renowned storyteller. He knew everything, and he especially liked to tell stories of the world of the past.

One day, he gathered the young ones around to tell them about humans.

"What's a human?" a young cockroach asked before the wise one could even begin his tale.

"Well, young one, you see, humans once ruled the entire world. They ruled all the other living things. All were made subject to them, but they let this poison their hearts. They became full of pride."

"What about cockroaches? Did they like cockroaches?" asked one of the listeners.

"Oh no, no they did not. They killed the cockroaches with poison, sprays, and traps. They despised us. We tried to stay hidden as best we could. We tried not to bother the humans. We had no qualms with them," the old cockroach explained.

"So what happened to the humans?" asked another listener.

"They destroyed each other with weapons much

greater than little spray cans and traps. They destroyed a lot of things with their weapons. They destroyed almost everything. Now we are all that remain. The cockroaches now rule the world. There is nothing else left alive, you see."

Blessed are the meek, for they will inherit the earth.

BLESSED ARE THOSE WHO
HUNGER AND THIRST FOR
RIGHTEOUSNESS, FOR THEY
WILL BE FILLED

THE HUNGRY KNIGHT

A great knight wandered the deserted land looking for food and drink. He had been on a long journey and lost his way. He could barely remember the mission and adventure that had brought him there.

He came across a small hut in the wilderness. It was quiet, but he saw the remains of a fire, and they were still warm.

"Hello," he called, "is anyone there?"

An old man came out of the hut, smiling peacefully, with arms outstretched in welcome.

Before the old man could speak, the knight said, "Old man, I have been traveling for a long time, and I am in great need of food and drink. Please, would you be so kind as to offer me something to satisfy my hunger and thirst?"

The old man nodded his head and turned back into his hut. A few moments passed, and he came out again with a small cup of water and some roots of a plant. He held out the gifts for the knight, keeping that same smile.

"Old man, is there any more?" the knight cried. "What have you to give me for my journey, for I have been traveling long and I am in great need of sustenance!"

The old man nodded once more and returned to his hut. Moments later, he emerged with a handful of dried fruits and gave them to the knight.

"Old man, there must be more. I have told you of my long journey!" With that, the knight came down from his steed and entered the hut. There he saw a bed, but nothing more. No food or drink was there to be spared. The old man had given him all that he had.

The knight went away angry, wandering aimlessly and hungry for a very long time.

The old man, however, was pleased by the company and felt gratitude for the gifts he was able to give to the knight.

Blessed are those who hunger and thirst for righteousness,
for they will be filled.

THE SUCCESSFUL BANKER

Fresh out of college, a young man was eager to find work and become very rich. He found a job at a bank and quickly learned some of the most devious ways to cheat people out of money.

He would convince families to take on loans they couldn't afford and earn commission on the sale. He would sell investments to men who risked their family savings to earn a big payout on attractive business deals.

The young man learned to say anything to get their money, and he did indeed become rich.

When Christmas came around that year, he celebrated dinner at home with his mother and brothers. They lived in a small town, and the mother had heard of all his business deals at the bank. The young man bragged about what he had learned and how he had made the money, hoping to impress his siblings. The brothers were impressed, but the mother was not.

She begged him to change his ways. She feared for his soul and the many people who had lost money because of him.

He left that night upset and angry that his mother was

so opposed to his success. The two didn't speak for a long time.

A few months later, a family came into the bank asking for help to pay for a loan that the young man had sold to them the year before. They told him how they could barely buy enough food to eat each month. The parents were very angry at the bank, but worst of all was the children. The children sat outside the young man's office with their heads down, sniffling with tears.

At the sight of the kids, the young man's heart was broken. He suddenly realized that all that time was wasted making money for himself. It was easy for him, but it was at the expense of so many others, whom he had fooled all this time.

He took the opportunity to legitimately help this family. He helped them negotiate better terms for the loan. He then began to help others make smarter investments. This earned him less money on commission but saved the people more money on the loans and investments.

He was much happier now. He didn't realize how good it felt to help others earn enough to be satisfied. Though he had less money now himself, he felt more satisfied than ever.

He asked for his mother's forgiveness, which she gave to him gladly.

Blessed are those who hunger and thirst for righteousness,
for they will be filled.

THE TATTLETALE

There was a young boy who had a reputation in his class as a tattletale. Anytime he saw anyone do anything wrong, he told the teacher or the principal. He thought everyone should always do the right thing, just like he did.

One day he saw a classmate steal a pencil from her neighbor. He immediately told the teacher, practically jumping out of his seat to make sure she got in trouble.

The teacher was shocked by the accusation. "Is that true, young lady?" she asked the girl, who was holding her neighbor's pencil.

"No! She let me borrow it," said the girl.

"She's right," said the neighbor honestly.

The boy was shocked. He felt awful for accusing someone who didn't do anything wrong.

He thought about this and realized that he hadn't considered the people that got in trouble because of him. He wanted people to get in trouble for doing something wrong. He had never thought much about how to help them do something right.

From that point forward, he stopped looking for people doing something wrong and started looking for people doing something right. He still told the teachers when he saw someone doing something to hurt someone, but he was mostly interested in seeing the good in others rather than the bad.

When he saw a good deed, he told a teacher. When someone said something nice, he gave that person a compliment. He was happier and had a lot of happy friends, too.

Blessed are those who hunger and thirst for righteousness,
for they will be filled.

THE HUNGRY DOGS

A family had two dogs, one old and very obedient dog and the other very young and untrained. One day, the family forgot to put food in their bowls before heading out to work and school. Both dogs were very hungry.

The old dog accepted this mistake and prepared for a long day. While he was hungry, he loved his masters and knew that they would surely feed him once they returned home. The young dog didn't like this at all. He was too hungry to wait all day for the food. He broke into the food pantry and ate everything he could.

At first he was full and happy, but then he felt sick and miserable. When the owners came home, they saw the pantry and the sick dog. They punished him and locked him in the back room, where he continued to feel very sick.

To the old, obedient dog, the owner gave a large number of doggy treats and a hearty dinner of dog food. He felt very full and grateful for the treats.

Blessed are those who hunger and thirst for righteousness, for they will be filled.

THE VACUUM

A vacuum sat very impatiently in the closet. It had lain there unused for a very long time. It feared the amount of dust and dirt that must have accumulated throughout the house. The owner of the house was very old and had let the house fall into disrepair and dustiness.

Winter came and then spring. Finally, the owner hired some help to care for the home. The mop, which sat next to the vacuum, was afraid. "What if we cannot clean up the mess?" it said to the vacuum.

"Even a little cleaner is better than not clean at all," said the vacuum. It was very excited to fulfill its purpose and greatly desired to inhale the dirt and dust.

Finally, the helper came and took the vacuum and the mop and the broom and all the other cleaning supplies out of the closet and began to clean the house.

When they were finished, they each felt satisfied, for they had rid the house of much dust and dirt. There was still more to clean, but it was much better than before.

Blessed are those who hunger and thirst for righteousness,
for they will be filled.

THE REFRIGERATOR AND THE PANTRY

The refrigerator and the pantry of a certain house were very concerned for their owners because of all the junk food and unhealthy things that they were eating.

"I can't do this anymore," the refrigerator said to the pantry. "I won't keep this junk food cool for them."

The pantry responded, "But fridge, you must keep the food cool. It is your purpose, and the family needs you."

"What shall we do, then, if we cannot force them to eat the right things?" asked the refrigerator.

The pantry didn't know the answer at first, but then it secretly rearranged the foods that the people stored inside of it so that the healthy foods could be seen first. The people still ate the junk food, but less than they had before.

The refrigerator saw this and said, "You have done well, pantry. If I had defied the family and refused to keep cool the unhealthy food, they would have replaced me."

The pantry agreed and said, "We can only suggest, not force them to do the right thing."

Blessed are those who hunger and thirst for righteousness,
for they will be filled.

THE THIEVES AND THE FAMINE

A great famine broke out throughout the land. People were hungry and starting to run out of food. They knew, however, that the church had a storage room full of food to give to the poor. They came demanding that the food be shared with them as well.

The pastor of the church came rushing out to stop them. "Don't you see?" He said. "This food is for the poorest of the poor. This is for those who have nothing. While you might be hungry, they are starving."

This didn't stop the mob. They pushed the pastor aside and raided the pantry. They left no food there for anyone else.

That night, many of the people ate the food that they had stolen from the pantry. Some of the others, though, realized that they had little, but that little was more than nothing. They felt remorse for stealing the food. They came back to the church the next day to return what they had taken.

There at the church's door were many poor and starving people who relied on the church for food. They were overjoyed to see the people returning what was stolen.

It was so little, but something was better than nothing for these poor people at the church's door.

The pastor welcomed the people back and forgave them. Those that returned could still feel their empty stomachs, but they felt better with full hearts.

Blessed are those who hunger and thirst for righteousness,
for they will be filled.

THE WANDERING WOLVES

A pack of wolves wandered through the forest searching for food. They found very little to eat and were becoming very hungry. There was a famine in the forest, so most of the animals had migrated to other forests, where there was more food.

The wolves hoped to find something in their forest, but they were unsuccessful day after day. Then they came across a farm on the edge of the forest, where a family of people had been able to maintain a large number of livestock.

Most of the wolves wanted to attack the farm, but one wolf disagreed. This wolf warned them not to attack and steal but instead to continue searching for food in this or another forest.

The wolves were too hungry to listen, and most of them attacked the farm. But a few others joined the wolf that wanted to do the right thing.

The attacking wolves were loud and slow from their awful hunger. The farmer saw them right away and shot at them with his gun. They were shot before they could steal and eat any animals at all.

The rest of the wolves continued wandering through the forest, following the one who had spoken up. They wandered for a few more days until indeed they found food again. First it was just a little, but then they found more than enough to eat. All it took was a little patience and trust that food would be found.

> *Blessed are those who hunger and thirst for righteousness,*
> *for they will be filled.*

THE OLD KNIGHT

An old knight purchased some land on a hill far outside of town. He had fought and won many battles in his time, which earned him quite a reputation. Alone on his hill, he intended to leave behind the life of a fighter and trade it in for the life of a farmer. He would grow enough food to feed himself without want or need for anything else.

But when the local town was overrun with evil magistrates, some of the townspeople came to visit the old knight to ask him for help.

Day after day, they came to plead for his assistance, and day after day, he declined to help.

Though the old knight liked to live in seclusion, he had to go to the town from time to time to shop for supplies and sell the crops from his farm.

There he witnessed for the first time the injustices done to the people of the town. They had become so poor that the town was filled with beggars.

The old knight started giving his food to the beggars in the street, but one of the evil magistrates saw this and demanded a tax upon the gifts.

The knight then realized his error. He had all this time

wanted happiness only for himself and ignored the needs of others. While he was able to feed himself with the produce from his farm, the many people of the town went hungry.

The knight paid the tax and gave the magistrate some of the food as well.

The next morning, a knight in armor that shined so brightly it seemed to glow in the morning sun arrived in the town, demanding to see the evil magistrates.

They feared him and would not come out of their homes.

Soon a crowd assembled behind the knight, ready for a fight.

No fight was necessary. The magistrates and their men moved on to another town.

The old knight became the protector of the town from that day forward, making sure everyone there could find work and food to feed their families.

Blessed are those who hunger and thirst for righteousness, for they will be filled.

THE SOCCER STANDOUT

A young boy had earned a reputation as a standout soccer player among the other kids his age. He loved to play the game. He had a soccer ball near him at all times. He was so good at soccer that he received an invitation to join the best travel team in his city, with the most successful coach in his age group's history. It was an honor to be invited to join the team.

At his first practice, the coach led them in the usual drills and ran through a few scenarios. Toward the end of practice, he taught the players how to slide tackle to steal the ball from the other team.

The boy was a little confused. "Coach, slide tackling like that is illegal."

The man laughed and said, "Only if you get caught." The other boys on the team laughed, too.

They had their first game the next weekend against a very difficult opponent. The other team had a reputation for really big and fast players.

"Remember that move I taught you at the end of practice," the coach reminded them before the game. "Slide and steal."

The boy heard this, and his stomach ached. He loved this game. He knew what the coach was telling them to do was wrong.

"Now get out there and win!" shouted the coach.

The team yelled and charged out into the field, except for the boy, who stood there on the sidelines looking up at the coach.

"I won't do it," he said. "I won't cheat."

"You won't get caught. Just get out there and listen to what I say," said the coach.

"No, I won't do it," he said in reply.

"Get out there now, or you are off the team," said the coach.

The boy looked to the field. Playing soccer was all he ever wanted to do, and this was the best team, with the best players. But he wanted to do what was right even more than he wanted to play soccer.

"I won't cheat," he said again.

"Then you can watch from the sidelines," said the coach.

During the game, his teammates did cheat, and they got caught. A few players were even ejected from the game. Then, when the coach tried to argue with the referees, he was ejected, too. Their team had to forfeit the game.

The parents were furious. They all pulled their kids off the team and joined other teams instead.

The boy found another team, too. It was a great team. They went on to win the city championship, and they didn't have to cheat to do it.

Blessed are those who hunger and thirst for righteousness, for they will be filled.

BLESSED ARE THE MERCIFUL, FOR THEY WILL RECEIVE MERCY

THE MERCIFUL FLOWERS

A daisy and a sunflower grew together out from under a stairway. They both needed the sun to grow, and there was too much shade under the stairs.

The sunflower was afraid of losing the sun, so it moved in front of the daisy to get more of the sun's rays. The daisy was sad and pleaded for its companion to share the sunlight so it, too, could grow.

The sunflower was afraid of the shade but felt bad for the daisy. It moved and shared the light equally so both flowers could grow.

The flowers grew to the height of the stairs, but a boy stomped on the sunflower while in a hurry to get up the steps. It fell to the ground under the stairway.

The daisy took pity on its companion, remembering how it had shared the sunlight when they were young flowers. The daisy moved itself into the shade so the trampled sunflower could get the sun it needed to grow again. The sunflower survived and—thanks to the help of the daisy— grew to become tall and beautiful once more.

Blessed are the merciful, for they will receive mercy.

THE ARMY OF THE FORGIVEN

Crime had become a big problem in a certain kingdom. The prisons were filling up with robbers who had stolen from the people near the castle. There would soon be no room for new criminals.

The king had a new idea for how to deal with this problem. He decided to do something unheard of. He showed the robbers mercy, freeing them and extending an invitation to fight in a special army on his behalf. They would be well fed and would have a purpose in life.

Thus, this special group of newly trained soldiers became known as the Army of the Forgiven. They had the king's trust and blessing as true knights to defend the kingdom.

This angered the people of the kingdom. While the king showed mercy, they showed scorn. They hated these men, and instead of calling them the Army of the Forgiven, they called them the Army of Thieves.

Shortly thereafter, a battle broke out in the kingdom. Most of the high knights and the king's guard were off fighting enemies in a different part of the kingdom, and only the Army of the Forgiven was there to protect the king and castle.

The attacking army snuck around the other armies to the castle. They were sure that they would be able to take the king, without soldiers to stop them.

Then the Army of the Forgiven emerged from the castle gate, ready for battle. Despite the men's intention to defend the kingdom, the people in the castle booed and hissed at them and shouted insults.

The people hiding in the castle placed no hope in the Army of the Forgiven, but the men knew they had the trust of the merciful king. They won a most glorious battle and defended king and castle.

Many men lost their lives in the battle, but those that survived returned not to scorn but to awe and respect.

These knights, who had received the mercy of the king, now felt the love and mercy of the people. Never again did they hear an insult or experience disrespect.

Blessed are the merciful, for they will receive mercy.

THE ANTS AND THE CHIPMUNK

There once was an ant that found the perfect spot to build a hill. He worked tirelessly, placing each grain of sand to carefully build his little home.

Unfortunately for the ant, he had built his home right at the top of a hole that was the entrance to the home of a chipmunk.

The chipmunk said to the ant, "Little ant, this is my home, and how will I enter without smothering your ant hill?"

The ant begged an apology. He asked for the chipmunk to show mercy and to let him keep his hill there at the opening of the hole.

The chipmunk relented. She dug another hole for her home, just a few feet away.

The next day, another ant showed up and built a home at the entrance to the new hole.

"Little ant," the chipmunk said, "I have just built this new entrance because your brother ant built his home in my other hole. Surely you can find another spot to build your hill?"

This ant, too, pleaded for mercy, and the chipmunk

relented. She found another spot to dig another hole to her underground home.

The next day, the chipmunk came out of her new hole to find many little ants busy at work, building homes all over the place. She had never seen anthills such as these. They were so high and strong and sturdy. She now had nowhere to create a new entrance to her home. She didn't know what to do.

Then the first ant came back and said, "Merciful chipmunk, we have something to show you."

The little ant and all his friends led the chipmunk to a hidden spot with perfect soil for building a new home under the shade of a tree.

"Please, could you give up your home and make a new dwelling here under this fertile ground?" asked the ant.

The chipmunk didn't like the idea of moving, but this land offered much more cover for any holes she might dig to a new home. She was merciful once again and gave the old land to the ants.

Not long after, the chipmunk's old home was flooded with water in a rainstorm. The water went right into the holes, giving the ants above some protection. The chipmunk's new home experienced the same storm, but it was on higher ground and did not flood like the first. The chipmunk's mercy for the ants had saved them all.

Blessed are the merciful, for they will receive mercy.

THE TREE IN THE PARK

A great tree stood in the middle of a park. Its branches grew high into the sky and also down close to the ground. Children loved to climb the tree.

There was a group of boys who had grown up climbing the tree. One of the boys, the leader of the pack, said, "Let's mark our names on this tree and claim it for ourselves."

So the boys carved their names in the tree. Then they did something awful. They painted it with spray paint. They broke branches and stripped it of its leaves.

The next day, no children came to climb the tree. It looked ugly and scary now that it was all mangled and painted.

One of the boys, the youngest, felt very bad about the damage that was done, but he was afraid to return to the park. He was ashamed.

He told the other boys so. They made fun of him. The boy said he was going to turn them in, and this made the others very angry. They began to chase him. The young boy ran as fast as he could until he saw the park. He ran straight to the tree and jumped into its branches.

The tree wanted to wrap its arms around this boy that it had loved for so many years as he climbed within its branches. It protected him from the other boys by hiding him in the leaves that remained.

Once the group gave up the search, the boy thanked the tree.

"You helped me even after I hurt you. You were merciful when I was mean. Please forgive me."

The tree seemed to stand a little taller that night. The boy vowed to take care of the tree and some day restore it to its original beauty.

Blessed are the merciful, for they will receive mercy.

THE BASKETBALL PLAYER

There was a very tall boy who was very good at basketball. He was also a good leader. When any of his teammates made a mistake or failed, he didn't get angry with them. Instead, he encouraged them and helped them get better.

It seemed like this tall young boy never made mistakes. The team always counted on him to make the winning shot.

When they played for the championship in the city tournament, the entire team was relying on him. He played well the whole game, but it was not enough. At the end of the game, the opposing team was ahead by one point.

He and his team had the final shot and a chance to win the game. His teammate passed him the ball, and he shot just as the buzzer went off to announce the end of the game.

The ball bounced off the rim and onto the floor. The game was over. They had lost.

The tall boy was very upset. He felt like he had let his team down. He thought they would be very angry with him because he lost the game for them.

When they got back to the locker room, every one of his teammates encouraged him. None of them was angry. All of them wanted him to know how grateful they were for his hard work and encouragement during the year.

"You always made us better players. You never got angry with us," they said to the boy.

Even though they lost, the team grew much closer together that year. They remained close friends for many years to come.

Blessed are the merciful, for they will receive mercy.

THE DUELING DOG AND CAT

A cat and a dog lived together in a house under the care of a good family. But the cat and the dog did not get along. They constantly fought and were often forced to be in separate parts of the house. It got so bad that the owners had to keep the dog outside.

This didn't stop either of them from trying to do mean things to the other. The dog would chase the cat anytime he saw her outside. He would bury her toys in the back-yard whenever he found them.

The cat would scratch the dog's toys in return, making them harder to chew.

Eventually, though, the dog realized that he could never come inside again unless he could learn to forgive and be kind to the cat. He dug up all the cat's toys and returned them to her. When the cat came outside, he let her roam free and never chased her anymore.

Without any mischief, the family let the dog back inside occasionally. He avoided the cat as much as possible and never did anything mean to her.

So the cat didn't ruin the dog's toys anymore. She was

a lot less angry and scared of the dog. Before long, the two animals got along just fine together, and the dog got to stay in the house all the time.

Blessed are the merciful, for they will receive mercy.

THE RAT AND THE RENT

A man and his daughter lived together in a run-down apartment. Lately, they had seen a rat running through the kitchen and bathroom. The father built a trap for the rat and caught him on the first try. He heard the trap catch the rat and went to go kill him, but his daughter got there first. She let the rat go free.

"Why would you do such a thing?" the father asked.

"He seemed so scared. I couldn't let him suffer like that, so I let him go," said the daughter.

This made the father very angry, but before he could say anything, there was a knock on the door.

The father unlocked the door and looked out into the hall. It was their landlord, who had come to collect this month's rent.

"I'm—I'm so sorry," said the father. "I don't have the money to pay right now, but I will. I promise I will have it next week."

This made the landlord very angry. He was ready to kick them out of the apartment immediately, but he saw the daughter standing in the back of the room. She looked very scared. The landlord's anger steadied. Then he saw the rat trap on the floor near the girl.

"Okay," he said to the father. "I'll give you one more week. I'll even lower the rate for the month. It looks like we have a rodent problem. You should have told me."

"Thank you," said the father. "I am so grateful."

"Thank you," said the girl.

Blessed are the merciful, for they will receive mercy.

THE KNIFE AND THE CUTTING BOARD

There was a knife and a cutting board that the people of the house used to prepare their food for almost every meal. The knife would cut through the food that was set on the cutting board.

The knife began to feel very bad for all the little lines it made on the cutting board. Over time, the cutting board did not look very clean or new anymore.

"I am so sorry," the knife said to the cutting board.

"You do not have to feel sorry," said the cutting board. "You are only doing what you are asked to do, and I am fulfilling my purpose, too. Do you not realize that your blade becomes more dull from scraping against my surface with each slice?"

The knife thought about this and realized the cutting board was probably right. They were both worn down after being used so many times.

So they each forgave the other. The knife forgave the board for dulling its blade. The cutting board forgave the knife for cutting into its side.

Blessed are the merciful, for they will receive mercy.

THE OLD TEDDY BEAR

A young girl had a teddy bear that she loved dearly. She carried him wherever she went. The bear loved her, too, and felt very proud to be by her side every day.

The girl carried that bear around so much that it started to wear and tear. The color faded, and the cotton inside either fell out or became so worn down that the bear wasn't so fluffy anymore. Buttons for the eyes were missing or falling out. The bear was no longer his old self.

Eventually, the girl grew older, and the bear was placed in the back of a closet for many years.

The bear could have been angry with the girl for taking such poor care of him, but he wasn't angry at all. He was so grateful for all the time he got to share with her. He loved her and forgave her for letting him fall apart. He wasn't even angry for being stored away in a closet, because he knew that meant she loved him enough to keep him instead of throwing him away.

Many years passed, and the girl didn't play with the bear anymore. She had grown up and no longer lived in the house.

Then one day, she came and found the bear in the

closet. It made her smile. She even hugged him. Then, she put him in a bag. Again, the bear could not be angry. He was so happy to be found again and to be loved by the girl.

When the bear was taken out of the bag, the girl, who was a woman now, began to repair him. She cleaned him and filled him up with new cotton stuffing. She sewed him up where there were holes. She sewed on a new button for his missing eye.

Then she did the greatest thing of all. She placed that little bear inside a small bed, where her young son was sleeping.

When he woke up, he started to play with the bear. He played with the bear quite often and carried him around wherever he went for many years to come.

Blessed are the merciful, for they will receive mercy.

THE MOTHER BIRD AND THE SQUIRREL

A mother bird was ready to lay her eggs. She left her newly made nest for just a short time so she could have one last meal before laying the eggs. She found a very fine worm and flew back to her tree, but just as she was about to land in her nest, she saw it tumble to the ground.

She looked around and saw a squirrel hopping along the branch in a hurry.

At first, the bird was furious. She was ready to attack that squirrel, but then she realized there was no time. She had to build another nest quickly, before her eggs could be laid.

Gathering twigs and grass from around the tree, she made her nest as quickly as she could. It wasn't perfect, but it was enough to lay her eggs.

With the nest built and the eggs inside, she sat down to keep them warm. Then she felt the nest, which had been built in a hurry, starting to fall, and her worst fear was realized. She scrambled out of the nest to try to keep it from falling.

The squirrel saw the mother bird trying to save her eggs. He climbed up the tree and along the bottom of the branch to hold up the nest. He nudged the nest back upright so that it was once again on a sturdy spot.

"Thank you so much!" cried the bird.

"Don't mention it," the squirrel replied. "I felt awful about knocking over the first nest, so I stuck around here to make sure you would be okay. When I saw your new nest falling, I just had to help."

"I don't know what I would have done if you had gone away," said the mother bird. "Thank you."

Blessed are the merciful, for they will receive mercy.

BLESSED ARE THE PURE IN
HEART, FOR THEY WILL
SEE GOD

THE EAGLE AND THE OWL

There was an eagle that liked to fly very high.

A wise old owl asked the eagle, "Why do you fly so high?"

The eagle replied, "I want to see the great Creator of the birds of the sky. I want to see God."

With that, the eagle looked to the sky and flew as high as he could. Higher and higher he flew, up and up until he could not pump his wings any more. He was exhausted and he began to soar back down to the trees below.

"I will work hard and become stronger," he said to himself.

He spent many days flying fast and over long distances to strengthen his wings. He did this for a very long time until, indeed, he was much stronger.

He looked to the sky again. He launched himself into the air and with renewed strength flew higher than any bird had ever flown before.

He looked around with his keen eyes, but he saw nothing but blue sky and the clouds below him. He could not see God.

He tried to fly even higher, but his wings gave up with

exhaustion once more, and he soared back down to the trees.

There he saw the wise old owl once more. "Eagle," said the owl. "Have you seen what you hoped to see?"

"No," replied the eagle. "There is nothing to see up there but blue sky and clouds."

The owl paused for a moment, then asked, "Must you fly high in the sky to see God?"

The eagle stared up at the sky but did not respond.

"You have been blessed with strength that took you higher than any other bird before. Who made you to be an eagle? Who made you to become so strong?"

The eagle's eyes came down from the sky and looked to the owl. He realized the owl was right, and that God had been with him all along.

Blessed are the pure in heart, for they will see God.

THE WORTHY WARRIOR

There once was a warrior who won many battles. He won much glory throughout the kingdom and was known and loved by all. Then one day he was defeated in battle. He came home without honor and was banned from his kingdom by the angry king.

The warrior was forced to wander in the wilderness, not knowing what to do with himself after his defeat.

One day the warrior was walking along the edge of a mountain when he saw a door. On the door, he saw one clearly written word: Worthy.

"Worthy?" he said to himself. "What does this mean?"

The warrior pushed the door with all his strength. It did not move. He took out his sword and tried to break it down, and still it did not move.

He tried and tried with everything he could think of, not sure why he was trying so hard. He sat down with exhaustion. He was ready to give up when he said:

"This cursed door speaks truth. I am not worthy. I am doomed to wander as a lost soul for the rest of my days. My might has not helped me. My sword has not helped me. I will lay it all down and leave it before this door for another worthy warrior to test his might instead. I will go from this place and become a lowly servant to live a simple life without honor or fame as the warrior I once was."

In that moment, there came from the door a loud boom, and it slowly inched open.

From inside the door and deep in the mountain came a light so bright the warrior had to cover and close his eyes.

When he opened his eyes and could see the light, he witnessed such beauty that his heart, which had felt so empty before, became now filled with joy.

The warrior went from this place a changed man. He served many people from that day forward, never seeking fame or reward but seeking only to help the ones who needed it most.

Blessed are the pure in heart, for they will see God.

THE SHAPE OF THE CLOUDS

A dad took his young daughter out on a daytime date. They went for a hike in the woods and came upon a clearing with a nice patch of grass. They laid down to rest and looked up at the sky.

There were hundreds of white, fluffy clouds floating overhead.

"What do you see in the clouds?" asked the dad.

"What do you mean?" asked the daughter.

"I mean, what do the clouds look like to you?" he said. "Like that one. I think it looks like a treasure chest."

"Oh, I see. Let me try," said the girl, thinking for a moment. "See that one over there? I think it looks like an angel."

"Is that so?" said the dad. "Well, I think that one over there looks like a fancy car."

The girl looked at his cloud and frowned a bit. "Yeah, I guess so."

"Well, what do you think it looks like?" he asked.

The girl hesitated for a moment. "Don't laugh," she said.

"I won't," said her dad.

"I think it looks like God," said the daughter.

"God? Really? And what makes you say that?" he asked.

"Well, I don't know. I mean, we don't know what God looks like or anything, but when I see that cloud, it makes my heart happy. All these clouds do. I can see a cross over there, and there's a mountain, like the one where Moses got the Ten Commandments. Oh, and there's Noah's Ark!"

"That's amazing," he said, looking at the happiness on her face.

The dad didn't see any of these things in the clouds she pointed to, but he was pleased to hear that she could see so many beautiful things that reminded her of God.

Blessed are the pure in heart, for they will see God.

THE BLIND BOY

A young boy, blind from birth, asked his parents to take him to a church. His parents never went to church. They were angry with God for taking away their son's sight.

Although they were confused by the request, they relented and brought him to a nearby church. It was empty. No one was there worshipping.

The family walked through the doors, and the son asked his parents to describe what they saw.

They told him about the empty pews and the stained-glass windows. They described the altar in the front of the church and the ambo where people read stories from the Bible. Then they told him about the statue of Jesus on the cross.

"What does the cross look like?" he asked his parents.

"Well," they said, "there are two wooden beams inter-secting. Jesus's arms are nailed to the smaller, horizontal beam, and his feet are nailed to the bottom of the cross, which would have been placed in the ground."

"What does Jesus look like?" he asked them.

"He has a crown of thorns on his head and a beard. He is looking down. He looks very sad about his death."

"Are you sure he is sad?" the blind boy asked his parents.

"Well, that's what it looks like to me," said the father.

"Look closer, Dad," said the boy. "That's not the way I picture him. I see a face full of joy in anticipation of what is coming next."

"And what is that?" asked the mother.

"Jesus died, but then he rose again. How could he be anything other than full of love and joy on the cross? He knew he would rise again."

The parents looked at each other with tears in their eyes.

"Mom and Dad," said the boy, "can we come back here again?"

"Yes," they both said to him. And they did.

Blessed are the pure in heart, for they will see God.

THE SUN AND THE TRAVELER

A traveler hurried along the road to the city ahead. He was in a very big rush and had left early in the morning. He was moving to a new home in the big city and leaving behind the life of a peasant in a small town. He had great dreams of becoming rich in the city.

As he traveled along the road, the sun began to shine so brightly he could barely see. In all his days, he had never seen the sun so bright. First he had to shield his eyes, and then he had to close them completely to keep from being blinded.

The light seemed to shine brighter and brighter with each step he took toward the city. He walked slowly and then eventually not at all.

When he turned away from the city, the light got a little less bright. He didn't know what to do. He wanted so desperately to make it to the city. He had a hard time letting go of his plans to be there by the end of the day.

The traveler had two options: go back or stay where he was until the sun went down. He knew that it was dangerous to be out along the road in the wilderness after dark.

That left only one path to take—the path home. He accepted this as his fate and returned home, able to see much better along the way.

From then on, he was content to live in his own small town as a simple peasant. He wasn't poor, but he was never rich. There in his home, the light shone brightly but not so bright that it blinded him from seeing the beauty that was right in front of him.

Blessed are the pure in heart, for they will see God.

THE PICTURE OF GOD

There was a little girl who loved to draw. She drew pretty pictures every day and often gave these pictures to her parents or her brother.

One day, she decided to draw a picture of God. She sat down and got out her markers, but she didn't know where to start.

"What does God look like?" she wondered.

She got up and found her brother and asked him what God looks like.

He pointed up to a picture of Jesus on the wall in their family room. "Look, he's got a beard and brown hair," her brother said.

"Not Jesus, I mean God," said the little girl.

"But Jesus is God," said the brother.

"Oh," said the girl.

"Why don't you go ask mom for help?" he said.

So she did. She found her mom in the kitchen, talking on the phone. "Mom, what does God look like?"

Her mom covered the phone and said, "Can this wait for just a few minutes?"

"Mom, how am I supposed to draw God?" she asked, ignoring what her mom said.

"I don't know. He's a Spirit, so it's pretty hard to draw," said her mom.

"Not the Holy Spirit. How do you draw God?" asked the girl.

"Sweetheart, the Holy Spirit is God. Why don't you ask your dad?" she said, and started to talk again on the phone.

So the girl went outside to find her dad and asked, "How do you draw God?"

Her father was busy in the garage, but he paused and looked to her. "Did you ask your mom?"

"Yeah, and my brother, too," she said.

"And what did they say?" asked her dad.

"They said to draw a picture of Jesus and the Holy Spirit," she said.

"Well, then there's just one more picture to add," he said. "You have to draw the Father. He is God, too."

The girl was very confused. Her dad smiled and went back to his work.

The girl went back inside and sat down again to draw her picture.

She picked up a marker, but this time, she closed her eyes and said, "Hey, God, what do you look like?"

She opened her eyes and smiled. Then she began to draw.

Blessed are the pure in heart, for they will see God.

THE FOGGY WINDOW

A great, wide window spanned almost the entire front room of the house. The window was very proud of the view it showed to the people in the house.

One year, there was a very cold and wet winter that created so much moisture that the window became quite foggy when the weather was warmer. The fog made it hard to see through the window into the outside world.

Then the people in the house invited a man over to inspect the window. This made the window very sad, for it feared that it would be replaced.

It recalled all the many beautiful sights it had provided for the people to see. It loved to show the people the many glorious sunsets. There were full moons and stars so bright they seemed to come alive. The gardens looked beautiful through the clear window. The window was grateful for helping the people of the house see these beautiful sights. It was honored to have been able to serve them all this time.

A few days later, the man returned, and the window prepared itself to be replaced. But to the window's surprise, the man fixed the glass instead. The window wasn't getting replaced; it was getting restored!

After some long, hard work, the glass was clear again and the people inside could now see the incredible beauty of the outside world.

Blessed are the pure in heart, for they will see God.

THE BLACK CONSTRUCTION PAPER

The black pieces of construction paper were always the last ones in the house to be used. This made most of the pieces of black paper very sad. They wished they could have been made like the other, more popular colors of paper, like blue or red.

There was, however, one sheet of black paper that felt hopeful and happy about its color. It knew that black was an important color. It felt confident that it would be used to create something beautiful one day.

A holiday arrived, and the kids in the house got out all the glue, crayons, markers, and construction paper they could find. First, the kids used the very last sheets of red, orange, and pink. They even used the last sheets of blue and yellow, which was odd for this holiday. Then a child picked up the black sheet of paper.

She placed the paper on the table, then poured glue all over the center of the page. She placed her heart-shaped creation in the center of the black sheet of paper. It was a beautiful sight to see.

Blessed are the pure in heart, for they will see God.

THE WIZARD'S GLASSES

A great wizard was tired of seeing all the ugliness in the world, so he decided to do something about it.

He found a pair of eyeglasses and put a spell on them. He intended for the spell to change the way people saw the world. Anyone who looked through the glasses would see only beautiful things. The ugliness around them would be turned into beauty.

He tried on the glasses and found that they worked. He saw many beautiful things around him. He wanted to share the glasses with others, in hopes that people would be more kind and loving if they saw only beauty around them.

So he took his glasses to the market at the center of the nearby town to test them out. He asked some of the people there to try them on.

The first person he asked was happy to help. She put on the glasses and smiled. Just like the wizard, she saw the beauty of the world around them.

The next person tried to avoid the wizard. He did not want to try on the glasses. "I don't trust you or your magic," he said. The woman was still there and convinced the man to try the glasses on anyway.

He put them on and choked in disgust. "All I see is ugliness," he said. He tossed the glasses back to the wizard and went away angrily.

A crowd had now gathered around them. They were all suspicious and hoping to cast the wizard out of the town as soon as possible. Some of them tried on the glasses and, like the man, saw only ugliness.

Person after person in the crowd tried them on in anger, and each one saw only ugliness around them.

This made the wizard angry, too. He took back the glasses and stormed out of the town.

"I will keep them for myself," he said, and put the glasses back on. But to his astonishment, he could see only ugliness around him, too.

"What is wrong with these things?" he said aloud.

Then, he realized what was wrong.

The woman who had tried them on first was happy. She had an open mind and an open heart and was able to see beauty all around her. The others didn't have open minds or hearts. They were angry. When they tried on the glasses, they saw only ugliness. Likewise, when he was angry, he saw only the ugliness in the world.

The wizard hid the glasses and never wore them again. He didn't need glasses to tell him how his inner thoughts and feelings influenced the way he saw the world.

Blessed are the pure in heart, for they will see God.

THE OLD MAN'S HEART

A well-respected, churchgoing man had fallen into some bad health. His wife, children, and grandchildren became very concerned. They convinced him to go see a doctor to find out the root cause of his illness.

The man loved his family very much. He would do anything for them. He went to the doctor, even though he didn't like being in the hospital. The doctor ran a lot of tests and brought the man and his wife in to talk about the results.

The doctor told the man that he had a very bad heart. He said they would need to do some extensive surgery. There wasn't a very good chance that he would survive.

His wife was in tears upon hearing the news, but the man seemed in good spirits still. She asked him why he wasn't angry or sad.

"The doctor said I had a bad heart. I found that funny. How can I have a bad heart when it is so full of love for you and our children and our grandchildren? How can my heart be bad when it is filled with the love of God?"

This didn't cheer up his wife very much at the time, but

she remembered the conversation many months later after the man passed away.

It was then that she told her children and grandchildren about what he had said. "His heart was full of love for you," she told them. "I have no doubt he is sitting before the Lord right now with that smile we all know and love."

Blessed are the pure in heart, for they will see God.

BLESSED ARE THE
PEACEMAKERS, FOR THEY
WILL BE CALLED CHILDREN
OF GOD

THE GREEDY SONS

A landowner had many sons. Each son loved his father's land and the fields very much. All of them wished to own the land for themselves.

The father went on a long trip and entrusted the land to his sons to care for while he was away.

The sons argued over which parts of the land would be theirs. They each wanted something that another son wanted, too.

They argued and argued for days, and then they began to destroy the fields so that their brothers would not be able to keep them. They each thought that if they could not have it for themselves, then no other brother should possess it either.

Meanwhile, the servants of the field, who loved the land and loved to take care of it, tried to save it. They put out fires and repaired the damages. They worked together to save what was brought to almost complete destruction by the sons.

The father returned and saw what his sons had done. "Who has ravaged the fields and almost destroyed the land?" he asked them.

At first, no one spoke. Then they each pointed to one another, blaming their brothers for destroying the land.

The father was very disappointed. He looked around and saw the many servants still working to fix what was broken.

"My sons, in failing to care for my lands, you have lost your share of the inheritance. Now, you will be the servants, and the servants will be my sons. They have restored rather than destroyed. For this, they will receive this great land when I die, because they have shown a love for it and for each other."

Blessed are the peacemakers, for they will be called children of God.

THE WOLF AND THE BEAR

Bear and Wolf did not like each other. Wolf was fast and ruthless. He liked to hunt with his other wolf friends. No other kind of animal was welcome among them.

Bear was big and strong. He was usually alone and liked to follow his routine every day. There were places he liked to eat, rest, and relax. The thing that angered him most was being bothered during his routine.

One day, Wolf wandered into the woods where Bear lay resting. Disturbed from his sleep, Bear stood in all his might to scare off the wolf. Wolf, however, wouldn't relent. He was angered by the threats of the bear and not intimidated by his size.

Wolf growled and bent his hind legs into position to leap, and Bear raised his claws, ready to strike the wolf in his attack.

To their surprise, neither was able to reach his enemy. Two vines from a tree whose branches stretched out above them came down and wrapped around the beasts. Wolf and Bear could not move. They snapped their teeth and growled at one another.

They stood there, trapped and staring at each other,

with anger rising greater and greater, yet the vines would not budge.

"Tree," Bear growled, "why have you imprisoned us so?"

"Yes," said Wolf. "Let us finish what we started!"

The tree did not respond. The vines edged Bear and Wolf closer together until they were almost touching one another.

The two animals were angry with each other, angry with the tree, and angry with themselves for being unable to escape the trap.

They continued to glare at one another, often growling or snapping but unable to reach the other.

Time went on and they became tired. The more they looked on the face of the other, the more each realized he was just as helpless as his enemy.

They each saw the weakness in the other—a weakness that they shared in this moment—and lost the desire to attack. In time, their anger turned to understanding, and the understanding turned their hatred into mercy.

Wolf spoke first this time. "Bear, there is one way for us to get out of this trap," he said. "We can free each other by each biting the vines from the other."

Bear had had the same idea, but he said, "How can I be sure you will not attack me once you are free?"

Wolf replied, "I now see our shared weakness. Though we have differences, we are brothers and share in this struggle. I vow never to attack you again."

"And I vow as well," said Bear.

Before the animals could chew through the vines, the tree let them both free.

Wolf and Bear thanked the tree and looked upon each other differently from that day forward.

Blessed are the peacemakers, for they will be called children of God.

THE ARTISAN OF PEACE

A father died and left his two sons his entire estate. The sons loved their father very much. They each wanted something important of his to remember him by. The problem was that they each wanted the same thing.

The father was an artisan and master of many crafts. One of his greatest talents was in simple woodworking. He carried one of his wooden creations in his pocket everywhere he went. It was this little sculpture that the two sons both wanted to keep more than any other possession of their father's.

After many days of arguments, the brothers grew more and more upset with each other. When it came to the pocket carving, they decided to cut it in half and divide it between them.

When they took their separate halves, they each decided never to see the other again. They felt they could never forgive one another. They went their separate ways and tried to live separate lives.

Life would have gone on this way for them if it weren't for the carving. When they each touched their half, they tried to remember their father, but all they could think about were their memories as brothers. The memories were so vivid that it was like reliving each moment.

They relived countless adventures they had had as children. They relived their favorite family memories and other little moments that they had not thought of in years. Memory by memory, they started to miss one another, sometimes even more than they missed their father.

Now they stayed away from each other because of guilt rather than anger. Each brother was afraid that the other would never forgive him for the way he had acted.

On the anniversary of the father's death one year later, the brothers came to visit their father's grave. Each had his half of the carving in his pocket.

Without realizing it, they both arrived near the grave at the same time. They each held the carving in their hands. The memories it shared now were not so nice. The brothers relived those many arguments after their father's death. The memories, though, were no longer filled with anger and hate. They were now filled with shame and sorrow.

Suddenly, they saw each other. What surprised them most was the expression they saw on each other's faces. They did not see anger or resentment. Instead, they saw true joy. They each were filled with joy at the sight of the brother before them. They were reunited at last and each immediately began to plead for the mercy of the other.

They forgave one another at that moment, and they expressed gratitude for the father's incredible carving, which had brought them back together both in body and in spirit. The brothers shared many more joyful memories in their lives, but they no longer needed the carving to relive them. All they needed was the company of the other and the willingness to remember.

Blessed are the peacemakers, for they will be called children of God.

THE FIGHTING PARENTS

A young girl's parents were arguing much more than usual lately. The yelling could be heard throughout their house. She was determined to make them stop.

First, she tried to yell, too. She thought she could yell loud enough to make them stop, but they just yelled back and sent her to her room.

Then she tried to insert herself into the conversation. She took sides and defended each of them against the other. That didn't work, either, because both of her parents were now angry with her, too.

Finally, she came into the middle of a fight and sat down in tears. She had nothing to say and knew of nothing else to do.

"I'm sorry," she said to them. "I don't know how to help you love each other again."

The parents looked at one another and then at their daughter.

"You don't have to be sorry," said the mother.

"It is not your responsibility to stop us from fighting," said the dad.

The girl looked up at her parents. "When I was

younger, you taught me how to say sorry. You taught me how to forgive. Forgiveness makes fights go away. Can you just forgive each other?"

The parents looked at each other with tears in their eyes and nodded their heads.

"Yes," they both said.

They fought a lot less from that point forward, and seldom if ever in front of their daughter. Now they tried to forgive first, before fights broke out.

Blessed are the peacemakers, for they will be called children of God.

THE DOG AND THE MAILMAN

There was a dog who lived in a nice house with kind owners. His owners had a baby who loved to take naps in the afternoon.

Every day around three o'clock, the mailman would bring mail to the house. From inside, the dog growled and barked and woke up the baby. The owners tried everything to make him stop, but nothing worked.

Then one day, a new mailman was assigned to the route. The dog seemed to bark even louder at the newcomer.

But this mailman did something different. He paused, smiled, and acknowledged the dog. He spoke kindly to the dog. As the days and weeks went on, he was even able to pet and play with the dog.

The dog no longer barked at the mailman. Instead, he jumped for joy when he saw him.

The owners thanked the new mailman frequently. They were so grateful that their baby was able to take an uninterrupted nap in the afternoons now.

Blessed are the peacemakers, for they will be called children of God.

THE WATER FAUCET

An old sink had a water faucet with two knobs, one for hot water and one for cold. Both knobs thought they were better than the other. They liked to loosen themselves ever so slightly so that more hot water or more cold water would come out.

The people of the house didn't notice at first, but as this battle went on, each knob would loosen itself more and more.

Sometimes too much hot water would pour out of the faucet, burning the hands of the people that used it. At other times, the water was too cold, and the people could not use it to properly clean and comfort their hands.

Finally, the faucet put an end to the battle. "My dear knobs," it said. "You must stop this. Sometimes the people come to us for hot water. At other times they look for the water to be cold. Still other times you must work together in order to offer just warm water—not too hot and not too cold. You must stop this or we will all be replaced."

The faucet was right, and the knobs knew it. The next day a plumber came to inspect the sink and the hot water.

The knobs worked together to offer exactly the amount of hot or cold water that was needed.

The plumber let the people know that there was no need to replace anything, and the knobs continued to work together from that day forward.

Blessed are the peacemakers, for they will be called children of God.

THE OLD FOX AND THE YOUNG FOX

An old fox sat near the river eating worms, mollusks, and berries.

A young fox came by and laughed at the old one. "Dear old fox, are you too old for the thrill of a hunt?"

The old fox replied, "No, young one. I still have energy enough to hunt, but I choose to live in peace instead. I am much happier today than before, and I live in harmony among the animals."

The young fox laughed and said, "Suit yourself."

The young fox went out hunting. He saw a rabbit and ran after him. He jumped to pounce on the rabbit, but the rabbit turned and ran another way, leaving the young fox to fall right into the river.

The current in the water was strong, and the river carried him a long way. He passed the old fox that sat peacefully on the shore and tried to cry out, but the old fox didn't hear him. The young fox continued to struggle as the water carried him very far away.

Blessed are the peacemakers, for they will be called children of God.

THE TERRIBLE KING OF THE JUNGLE

A great and terrible lion ruled the jungle. All the other animals feared him, and few ever spoke out against him.

In time, the subjects of his kingdom could no longer bear to be ruled in fear. A great and brave tiger came to wage war against the lion. He challenged him in a fight for the throne.

All the animals of the kingdom, including the lion's son, were there to witness the great battle. The lion and the tiger fought ferociously, but the lion had the upper hand. The tiger begged for mercy, but the lion did not give it to him.

With a fatal blow, he took the life of the tiger. He turned to all those watching and pronounced, "Thus always to those who oppose me!"

The son of the king was very upset. He was great and mighty himself, but he would never rule a kingdom in fear like his father.

He ran onto the battlefield to oppose his father. He told him that he did not deserve to be king any longer, and the crowds of animals cheered in agreement. The king of the jungle roared, but his son did not flinch.

"You oppose me? Then you will no longer be called my son!"

The son said, "How can I be the son of a tyrant? I will not let you treat these animals like this."

The father roared again and launched to strike his son. The son dodged the attack and the father plunged face first into the ground. The king shook off the dirt and turned to attack the son again. But he was not alone. All the animals of the kingdom stood at his side, ready to defend him.

"Long live the king!" they shouted, referring to the son.

With a growl and a deep roar, the old king charged for another attack, but he was outnumbered. The animals fought back and chased off the old king. Now they served a new king, the peacemaking son of the old tyrant.

Blessed are the peacemakers, for they will be called children of God.

THE PEACEFUL TOWN

There was a war going on, and the people of a small town wanted to have no part of it. They enjoyed their peaceful life and didn't care much which side of the war won.

They were able to enjoy their peace for a long time, but eventually the battles came nearer and nearer to their town.

Some soldiers arrived one evening, seeking shelter after a long battle. The townspeople took pity on them and welcomed them in to feed them and treat their wounds.

Later that evening, another group of soldiers came seeking shelter. They were of the opposing side, but the townspeople didn't know this. They welcomed them, fed them, and treated their wounds, just like the first group.

There the soldiers got a good night's rest. They awoke in the morning wearing plain clothes that the peaceful townspeople had given them.

All the soldiers from both sides came to eat together at the local town square. They didn't recognize their enemies. They just assumed that those they didn't know were from the town.

The soldiers got to know one another and liked each

other very much. They didn't suspect that they were becoming friends with their enemies.

A few days later, all of the soldiers decided it was time to return to the war. They put on their uniforms again and prepared for the battle.

When they were all about to depart from the town, both sides saw the other and realized they had been making friends with the enemy all this time.

Upon realizing this, they might have attacked immediately, but they didn't. Instead, they greeted one another and gained new respect for each other.

From that day forward, the two groups of soldiers fought for duty to their cause and honor alone, and not for hatred of their enemy.

Blessed are the peacemakers, for they will be called children of God.

THE BATTLE OF BROTHERS

An old man had two sons. He had been a great warrior in his younger years, and the people across the land told stories about his amazing deeds. His two sons grew in strength and courage like their father. They both seemed equally matched in their potential for greatness.

When they had both come of age, they approached their father to ask for his blessing on one of them as his heir. They each wanted to earn his special approval, admiration, and honor.

"You must show me you are worthy of this request," said the father. "I am not yet ready to bestow this honor on either one of you, not until you have proven yourselves."

Each of the brothers wondered how they could prove themselves. They reached the same conclusion and both prepared for battle. They obtained the best weapons of the land and trained themselves for a fight.

After weeks of preparation, the brothers declared a day for a duel between them. Neither one of them had spoken to the other during this time. They loved one another, but they each wanted to earn their father's blessing.

The day for the battle arrived, and the two brothers

put on their armor and weapons. They arrived on the battlefield, ready to attack.

People from the surrounding villages and towns gathered to watch. There was a large crowd forming now around them. They all wanted to see what the sons of such a great warrior could do in battle.

Then the father arrived. His expression was stern. The brothers could not tell what he was thinking.

It was time for the fight to begin. The two brothers, who loved each other greatly, stared at one another, each eyeing his opponent for weakness.

Then the younger brother set down his sword. He took off his helm and said, "Brother! What are we doing? I would not fight you for a thousand blessings."

The older brother turned to look at their father, who continued to watch intently. He gripped his sword tighter and charged toward his brother with his weapon raised.

In a flash, the older brother was knocked to the ground. His sword went flying, and his face hit the dirt. When he looked up, he saw his father standing over him.

"You have failed me, my son," he said. "The one who has made peace will have my blessing. Do you not know why I have lived without weapon or armor all these years? It takes more strength to make peace than to make war."

The father turned to his younger son. "To you, my son, my peacemaker, I give my blessing. You will be my heir and care for all that we now have together. You have earned my respect."

Then he helped the older son to his feet and brushed him off. "It is not too late, my son, to make peace."

The older brother nodded and set aside his helm. He walked up to his younger brother and grasped his hand. "You were right, brother. I pledge my allegiance to you."

Blessed are the peacemakers, for they will be called children of God.

BLESSED ARE THOSE WHO
ARE PERSECUTED FOR
RIGHTEOUSNESS' SAKE,
FOR THEIRS IS THE
KINGDOM OF HEAVEN

THE JANITOR

Every night, a janitor kept the bathroom of an office building spotlessly clean. It was so clean that the men who used it during the day thought it strange. They started to leave the bathroom messier and messier to see what would happen. They left toilet paper on the ground. They drew pictures on the bathroom walls.

But each new day that came, the bathroom was spotless, again and again.

The men began to write mean notes to the janitor. These notes were cruel, yet the bathroom and notes were wiped clean day after day.

Then one day, the boss came in to see his employees writing on the walls of the bathroom. He punished the men by firing them from their jobs. Before the men left, though, they laughed about their notes and how the janitor always cleaned up the mess.

The boss decided to stay late to apologize and thank the janitor. He came to the bathroom to find an old man scrubbing the cruel notes off the wall again.

"Excuse me," said the boss. This startled the janitor. He was focused on his intense scrubbing.

"Yes, sir?" said the janitor.

"I came to apologize on behalf of my employees. What they did was wrong, and I am sorry that you had to experience it. They have been released from their jobs."

"Thank you, sir, but that was unnecessary."

"Unnecessary? They were cruel to you and mocked you for cleaning this place so well each day. Why didn't you report them?"

"It is my job to keep the bathroom clean, not to change the way others act," he said.

"But they might never change," said the boss.

"No, they didn't, at least not yet. I would have gone on cleaning and scrubbing their cruel words for a long time. I would have scrubbed as long as necessary. Maybe, though, just maybe, they would one day realize their error and help keep this place clean as well."

"Why do you do it?" asked the boss.

"It is the right thing to do. That is all that is asked of me," replied the janitor.

The boss thought the entire next day about this conversation. Those words seemed to echo in his mind: "It is the right thing to do."

The next night, the boss returned again to find the janitor cleaning the bathroom once more.

"I'm giving you a raise and appointing you as the overseer of the upkeep of the entire building. It is yours to care for, with many others to train and teach."

The janitor said only one thing: "Thank you."

He inspired many people who got to know him in the years he worked there. He was always teaching the people who worked with him to seek to do the right thing no matter what others do or say to you.

Blessed are those who are persecuted for righteousness' sake, for theirs is the kingdom of heaven.

THE TURKEY WILD AND FREE

There was once a turkey that wanted to be free. The other turkeys laughed at his wish for freedom and insulted him. These turkeys were comfortable on the farm. They had plenty of food and shelter. The weather was getting colder now, and they all got very fat and slow. Almost none of them wanted to leave the comfort of the farm.

This one turkey had always felt the desire for freedom. The farmer's food was very nice, but it just didn't feel right. He didn't feel like he belonged there. He felt a strong desire to go to the woods in the distance, away from the farm.

Then one day, the farmer accidentally left the gate ajar after bringing food to the turkeys.

It was his chance. The other turkeys, gobbling up their food, saw him walk toward the gate.

"There goes that turkey, always wanting to be free," said one of the other turkeys.

"He thinks he's a farmer," said another.

"He can't take care of himself. He will starve," said a third turkey.

"Look how small he is now," said a very fat turkey. "We

are all very plump and happy. He is skinny and silly."

The closer he got to the gate, the more the turkeys laughed at him.

But he didn't listen. He took off in a sprint, running from the safety of the farm and the plentiful food that the other turkeys enjoyed.

He ran as fast as he could. He ran through the gate and out into the fields between the farm and the forest.

But then he doubted himself. He slowed to a halt as he was about to walk into the woods.

Maybe the other turkeys were right. Maybe he couldn't make it alone. Maybe he would starve and die out in the woods. He was just a plain old turkey, anyway.

He slowly went back to the farm. When he came close, he saw that now the farmer and his workers were taking the turkeys away, starting with the biggest and fattest.

One by one, the turkeys were all taken away. Tom didn't want to find out what happened next.

He went running again back into the woods, this time faster than ever.

Then he heard them. Turkeys who spoke differently than the ones he grew up with on the farm.

These turkeys sounded happy. They were running and flying. He had only ever known turkeys that sat and walked. These turkeys were running and talking and . . . free!

He went running with them, feeling full of joy that he wasn't alone.

They took him in and taught him how to be a wild turkey. He never went hungry and never felt alone again.

He lived through the winter with the turkey tribe of the woods, as free as can be.

Blessed are those who are persecuted for righteousness' sake, for theirs is the kingdom of heaven.

THE PAINTED WALL

A famous painter arrived in a very small city. The people wondered why he had come there, until one morning, he started to paint the wall outside the city.

He worked for many long years, painting a beautiful collection of scenes depicting good and holy men and women. He continued painting this masterpiece until he died as an old man, when it was nearly finished.

At first the wall was a sight for many travelers to come and see. They were amazed by the beauty of the painting and inspired to live with joy and in service of others.

As the years passed, though, some people began to paint over it to make fun of the images. Faces were replaced with silly smiles and monster heads. Entire parts of the painting were covered with black paint so that it was hard to see what the painter meant to express through his art.

This went on for many years, until one day, a young woman came to clean and restore the painting. She worked tirelessly to clear the monster faces and black splotches.

In the evenings, she would go home to rest, and sometimes when she returned in the morning, the parts of the painting she had restored were ruined again.

Day after day, she worked toward the restoration of the art. And day after day, her restoration was undone.

Soon the people began to laugh and make jokes about her. They called her crazy and cursed her for wasting her time.

A young boy came up to her one day and asked her why she was doing it. Why did she show up every day to restore the painting?

No one had asked her this before.

"What do you see when you look at this work of art?" she asked him.

The boy thought for a moment. "I don't know. I guess I never really looked at it before."

"Will you look now?" the woman asked.

"Yeah, I guess I will," said the boy. He looked closely at the painting and tried to see the original work of art. He had walked past the wall many times but never taken the time to really look at it.

Now it was like seeing it for the first time. He saw the art behind the graffiti and felt inspired. The art made him happy. He was filled with joy and hope for the world.

The woman had stopped her work and watched the boy. Soon the boy realized she was looking at him. He looked up with a tear in his eye.

"Do you see now? That is why I do this work."

Blessed are those who are persecuted for righteousness' sake, for theirs is the kingdom of heaven.

THE DOWNSTREAM SALMON

There was a salmon who lived in the ocean. Every summer, she and the other salmon would return to the rivers to swim upstream and find a home to lay their eggs

One summer, this salmon did something unexpected. She turned and started to swim back downstream, in the opposite direction from all the other fish.

As she swam, she started to bump into other fish. At first, this may have seemed like an accident, but then it was clearly getting in the way of the fish trying to swim upstream.

Some of the other fish were angry with her for turning and swimming in the wrong direction. Other fish laughed at her for going the wrong way, calling her stupid or a coward. But this little salmon swam on down the river, more determined than ever.

Surprisingly, some of the other salmon saw her determination and started to follow her. They started to swim downstream, too.

One by one, more fish followed her in the opposite direction from all the others. They didn't know why, but they were inspired by the determination of the first salmon to swim downstream.

Not all of them turned away, though. Many stayed with the pack and continued their journey upstream. They did not know that danger lay ahead for them. First, a family of bears came into the river and started to catch and eat the fish. Then, past the bear family, there came an even worse fate. The fish who had continued swimming upstream were captured in a giant net and taken away out of the water by fishermen.

The salmon who swam the wrong way felt compelled to find a new home to lay her eggs. She turned down an unknown river bend and there found a spot where she could spawn unharmed. Those that followed her found this new home delightful and thanked her again and again for leading them away from the danger.

Blessed are those who are persecuted for righteousness' sake, for theirs is the kingdom of heaven.

THE DISOBEDIENT DOGS

There was a group of dogs in a dog training class who vowed never to listen to their owners. They made a pact to ignore all human commands. They wanted freedom.

The owners didn't like this at all. The trainer said it was the hardest group of dogs she had ever tried to train. Nothing seemed to change their mind.

Then the smallest of the dogs grew tired of all the punishment for not listening. She started to respond to the commands and listen to the trainer and her owner. The other dogs barked at her and called her a traitor. They said mean things to her, but she remained obedient.

After a few training sessions, this little dog was honored before the entire class, and her owner was given a certificate. The dog graduated from training and didn't have to return again. The other dogs saw what she had earned and felt bad for their pact of disobedience. They started to listen to their owners' commands, too, and soon they were all sent home happily as well.

Blessed are those who are persecuted for righteousness' sake, for theirs is the kingdom of heaven.

THE OLD T-SHIRTS

There was a drawer of t-shirts that loved nothing more than to be worn all the time. Each shirt loved to give their owner joy and comfort during the day and at night.

One day, the owner of the shirts went on a shopping spree and bought a bunch of new, clean, and comfortable shirts.

The new shirts made fun of the old shirts, calling them ragged, faded, and overly worn. They claimed to be better than the old shirts. But the old shirts didn't listen. All they wanted to do was make their owner happy.

Eventually, though, the old shirts started to think the new shirts were right, because they didn't get worn nearly as much any more. Time passed, and they remained in the drawer. Eventually they were put in a cardboard box. The shirts were very sad about being removed from the drawer and stored away.

Then one day, the box was opened and the shirts were all laid out across the floor. The shirts all feared that they would finally be thrown away or, worse yet, used as rags.

The owner had scissors. She began to cut the shirts. The shirts were so very sad. The new shirts had been right all along. But the old shirts had given this person so much joy. Why were they hated and being destroyed?

The owner cut the shirts gently into squares. Then she used a sewing machine to connect the shirts together, until finally each shirt had become part of a new creation: a very soft and comfortable blanket, which the owner used every single night. The shirts were not forgotten. They were transformed into something new and more comfortable than ever.

Blessed are those who are persecuted for righteousness' sake, for theirs is the kingdom of heaven.

THE CARRIER PIGEON

A carrier pigeon flew as fast as he could through the air. He had been given a very important message to deliver, and there was no time to waste.

He grew tired, however, and found a nice spot with a fountain in the square of a city to rest.

The other pigeons there laughed at him. "Why do you serve the people and deliver those little notes? Here, the people serve us. They feed us seeds or the scraps from their meals, and we eat heartily. We are free, while you are a slave."

The carrier pigeon saw the food that the pigeons were feasting on and fighting over. He shook his head. The people fed them scraps. This was no feast at all. He ignored their mocking and continued on his very important journey.

When he delivered the message, the recipient was overjoyed. She fed the bird with the finest foods and treated him with the greatest of care.

Blessed are those who are persecuted for righteousness' sake, for theirs is the kingdom of heaven.

THE HUNGRY MICE

A pack of mice lived in the barn behind a house. Half of these mice became very hungry and were angry about their food supply. They wanted the food in the house that the people were eating. The other half of the mice knew that although the people food was better, their place was outside in the barn.

The hungry half made fun of the others. They called them cowards and weak. Meanwhile, they planned their entry into the house.

The day came, and the mice snuck into the house through a series of small cracks and holes in the wall. The other mice stayed in the barn, eating the crumbs outside.

At first, the mice in the house were successful. They broke into the pantry and filled their bellies with delicious food. But this made them very slow in their escape. The cat caught some of the mice. The rest were caught in mouse-traps. The mice in the barn knew that the hungry mice got what they deserved, and they never saw them again.

Blessed are those who are persecuted for righteousness' sake, for theirs is the kingdom of heaven.

THE MOTHER HEN AND THE FOX

Every night, a fox snuck into the chicken coop and stole a few eggs to eat for himself. The chickens were too afraid to stop him, so this went on for a very long time.

Then a mother hen decided one morning that she had had enough. She said to the other chickens, "I will stand for this no longer! This fox is a thief. He is taking our eggs! We must do something about it!"

One of the other hens said, "Hush! We may lay the eggs, but they belong to the farmer anyway. If we speak up or try to stop the fox, he will surely eat us instead."

All the other chickens agreed, because of their fear of the fox. This mother hen, though, did not listen. She wouldn't stop talking about doing something to stop the fox.

"You are a fool," said some of the chickens. Others chased her out of the chicken coop so they didn't have to listen to her anymore.

That night, the mother hen knew she had to do something. When the fox arrived to steal the eggs, she ran after him in a loud scurry. She clucked as loud as she could and waved her wings to chase the fox away.

She expected the other chickens to follow her and be loud, too, but they stayed quiet in their fear. The mother hen was on her own.

The fox laughed and dropped the eggs to the ground. He showed his sharp teeth and made ready to pounce on the mother hen.

"You fool," said the fox. "Now I will eat you!"

But before he could attack her, the farmer arrived. He had heard the loud noises of the mother hen and come to investigate. He saw the fox and chased him away.

He saw the brave mother hen and said, "Thank you! If it weren't for you, I never would have known this fox was here. Next time he comes back, I'll be here to catch him. No one is going to steal our eggs."

The mother hen felt very proud of what she had done. The farmer took a liking to her and let her roam free in the yard by the house to play with his kids, while the other hens stayed in the coop, laying their eggs.

Blessed are those who are persecuted for righteousness' sake, for theirs is the kingdom of heaven.

THE FIRST POST

A young girl was finally allowed to create an account on social media. Her parents asked her older sister to help her set up an account. They wanted their youngest daughter to fit in and make friends with the other girls at school.

The older sister helped the young girl get set up on the website and create an account.

"Now it is time to create your first post," said the older sister.

"I am so excited," said the young girl.

"What do you want to post about?" her sister asked.

The girl thought for a moment, then she started to type. She wrote about how much God loved her and how she loved him back. It was a very honest and heartfelt post to share.

Before the sister could stop her, the young girl clicked publish.

"What was that?" asked the older sister.

"What do you mean?" said the young girl.

"That's not the kind of thing you share with people online," said the older sister.

"Why not?" asked the girl.

"Because people won't follow you. They won't like your posts. They will ignore you, or worse, make fun of you for posting stuff like that. Delete the post quickly before someone sees it."

"No," said the girl. "I absolutely won't do that."

"Why not?" asked her sister. "What if people don't like you?"

The girl thought for a moment. "No big deal," she said. "I want to make God happy. Who cares if kids don't like my post because of that?"

They looked back at the computer and saw that the post had gotten its first like. Then another one, and another.

This made the older sister think for a moment about the kinds of things she was posting. She decided to follow her younger sister's example and post more things that would make God happy, without worrying what other people think.

Blessed are those who are persecuted for righteousness' sake, for theirs is the kingdom of heaven.

ABOUT THE AUTHOR

Jared Dees is the creator of *TheReligionTeacher.com*, a popular website that provides practical resources and teaching strategies to religious educators. A respected graduate of the Alliance for Catholic Education (ACE) program at the University of Notre Dame, Dees holds master's degrees in education and theology, both from Notre Dame. He frequently gives keynotes and leads workshops at conferences, church events, and school in-services throughout the year on a variety of topics. He lives near South Bend, Indiana, with his wife and four daughters.

Learn more about Jared's books, speaking events, and other projects at jareddees.com.

amazon.com/author/jareddees

facebook.com/jareddeesauthor

instagram.com/jareddees

twitter.com/jareddees

youtube.com/thereligionteacher

ALSO BY JARED DEES

Jared Dees is the author of numerous books, including another
short story collection titled *Tales of the Ten Commandments*.

Download a collection of these stories at

jareddees.com/tencommandments.

Other books by Jared Dees:

31 Days to Becoming a Better Religious Educator

To Heal, Proclaim, and Teach

Praying the Angelus

Christ in the Classroom